RAVAGE

UNTAMED SONS MC - BOOK 1

JESSICA AMES

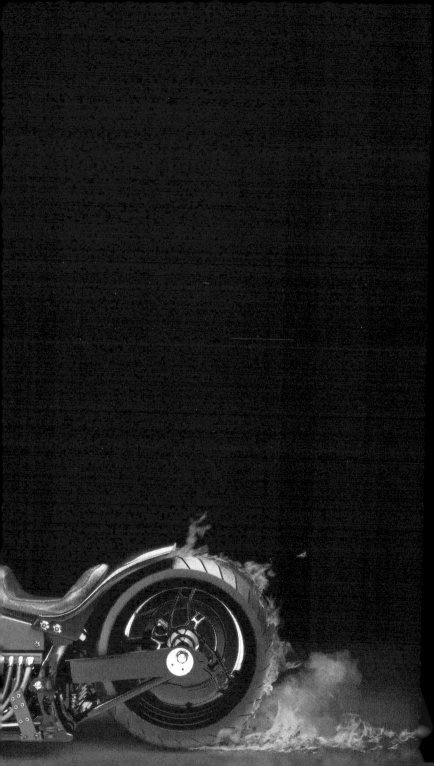

RAVAGE

UNTAMED SONS MC BOOK ONE

JESSICA AMES

AUTHOR'S NOTE

This book contains themes of rape, child illness, murder, mayhem and other topics that may be upsetting. Reader discretion is advised.

To Raven, who made this book better.

Ravage

Verb: cause severe and extensive damage to.

RAVAGE

Screams mean different things. Over the years, I've learnt to recognise their sounds, and what they signify by the timbre alone. Judging by the squealing this dumb fuck is making, Fury's having a little more fun than he should be. Time to wrap it up. My sergeant-at-arms can get carried away at times and if I don't rein him back in…

Well, dead men can't talk.

I push a booted foot off the wall and straighten, pulling my kutte back into place. I'm readying for the fight I know I'm about to have because once he's out of the box, Fury doesn't like going back in it. I used to think history was fun when it talked about berserkers—men hungry on bloodlust, so lost to it they didn't know their own names. Seeing it first-hand, it's a different ball game. Breaking through Fury's fury is never easy, but I need Frankie breathing, which isn't on the cards with Captain Bloodlust dealing from the deck.

As I cross the room, my footsteps loud on the concrete, the stench of copper is heavy in the air. It mixes with the thick, cloying smell of urine. The bastard must have pissed himself. Then again, if Fury was waving that pig-sticker around and carving bits off me, I might not think twice about pissing myself too—especially if I was hung up from the ceiling by my wrists and surrounded by men from a club with one of the darkest reputations around.

The Untamed Sons are not just my club, they're my brothers. We don't share blood, but our bond is deeper than that. We're bound by a different kind of sanctity. I trust each and every one of them to have my back, as I would have theirs. I'd bleed for them, just as they would me, because that is what club is. It's being part of something bigger than you.

It's also taking fucking orders.

I glance across the room towards Daimon, who's leaning against the wall, a cigarette hanging out of his mouth, his expression blank despite the scene in front of him.

"Day." I snap out his name and his eyes raise to meet mine.

I'm going to need his help. I'm a big bloke at six-five, but Fury's got a taste of the rage in him, and bringing him down when his bloodlust is flaring is not going to be easy.

Daimon stubs out his cigarette. His shaggy dark hair falls into his eyes when he lowers his head and he has to brush it back out of his face when he looks up again, ready to do what I need.

Fury makes a guttural groan as Frankie squeals.

Shit.

I twist back around and snag Fury's wrist just in time to stop him slamming his knife right between Frank's ribs. Glassy eyes slide up towards me. His face is covered in blood, sticking to his eyebrows, to his beard. His bare chest is blood spattered, and clean. He doesn't have a scrap of ink on him, other than the Untamed Sons insignia between his shoulders. They had to sedate him to do it. The guy might bleed a man without a second thought, but he's shit-scared of needles.

"Why'd you stop me?" he asks, as if I just walked in on

him balls deep in a club bunny, not bleeding Frankie, but then Fury has always got off on blood and pain.

"You remember the talk we had?" I hiss at him.

Daimon strategically hovers at his back, ready to strike out if necessary, which I'm grateful for. I can manage Fury on my own, but it doesn't hurt to have a little back up.

Fury doesn't make any attempt to move, though. He just stands still, his blood-crusted brows drawn together.

"I got carried away." I watch the demons sink back down, the blue of his eyes returning. He drops the blood-soaked knife on the floor and Day picks it up.

I squeeze his shoulder letting him know it's okay.

"Go and grab a smoke."

"Boss—"

"Not up for negotiation, Fury. You're done."

He looks disappointed, which doesn't surprise me. He has an astonishing work ethic for a psychopath. I watch him leave the room before my attention goes back to Daimon, who merely shrugs.

"You patched that crazy fucker in," is all he says as he pulls out his packet of cigarettes and lights a new one.

He's not wrong, but even so, would it kill him to be a little more supportive?

With a sigh, I turn back to my current predicament: Frankie Germain. I shrug out of my kutte, hanging it on a hook near the door. Time to get to work.

TEN MINUTES, and eight cracked and bleeding knuckles later, I emerge from the basement with the answers I need. Daimon exits behind me, the smell of nicotine following him as we step out from the pits of the clubhouse. I lock the door behind us and wait for him, watching as he scrapes his hair into an elastic band at the nape of his neck.

"Let him stew down there for an hour or two, see if he'll spill anything else. Then find Levi and Titch and get rid of our problem."

Get rid of Frankie, I mean. He's a liability. Arsehole knows too much and he's got a big mouth.

I know he'll do what I ask, so I don't wait for his agreement. Instead, I head down the maze of corridors to the common room and push through the doors. When I step into the bar area of the clubhouse, I'm hit with the heavy bass of some old rock tune and the din of voices talking over the music. It's noisy tonight. Then again, it's noisy most nights. My brothers like to party and they like to do it hard and loose.

I head for the bar, ignoring Noelle who tries to climb me like a tree as I pass her. Usually, I'd give the tiny half-naked blonde some attention, but tonight, I'm not in the mood. She must sense this, because she backs away quickly, moving on to find another target. I should feel bad, but I don't. She's just another club bunny wanting to get her teeth into a biker. They're all the same. They want a taste of rough and my boys are more than happy to give it to them—for the night at least. You don't take bunnies home.

I slide onto the first empty stool at the bar and raise two fingers to crook at the prospect behind it. Kyle is barely eighteen and he peers at me with eyes as black as his fucking soul and as dark as his skin. I like the kid, though. He's tough as nails and he'll make a hell of a brother—if he survives the prospect term.

Sin, my vice president, right hand and my little brother, found him at an underground fight club. He's got a lip piercing that I suspect my road captain, Titch, did pissed up one night. He's quiet and unassuming—unless he's fighting. Then, he's a demon.

He strides over to me, tossing the towel he was wiping the bar with on the side.

"Whiskey, kid. Make it a home measure."

Kyle nods and goes to make the drink. I lace my fingers together on the bar and glance around the room. This is my kingdom, my domain. It's a beat-up shithole of a place that smells of weed, cigarettes, stale beer, and pussy, but it's mine. I fought and bled to win and keep this slice of London. This patch of town belongs to the Untamed Sons and I'll bury anyone who tries to take it from me. I've buried more people than I can count over the years who thought different.

A tumbler with four fingers worth of amber coloured liquid in the bottom is slid in front of me. I lift it in salute at my bartender.

"Cheers."

It's about an hour later and another two tumblers of whiskey before Daimon comes to sit next to me. He orders a pint, before he says, "It's done."

I don't respond. There's no need to. I knew it would get done because I know my men. They're loyal to a fault.

Which is why I go on alert when a ripple of discomfort goes through him before he rubs the back of his neck uncomfortably. Day's smaller than me by maybe a couple of inches and I've got brawn on him as well—hardly surprising, I'm usually the biggest fucker in any room—but Daimon's a decent fighter and he's not someone to underestimate. I might be larger, but I have no doubt in a fight we'd be evenly matched.

"What?"

"There's a small issue…"

If he's fucked something up, I've no problem taking a fist to his face. He'll have no problem letting me either. That's the way of our world. The dynamic power balance that keeps things in check. The plod thinks we're a bunch of disorganised thugs that ride bikes and peddle powder. They couldn't be more wrong.

He doesn't say anything, despite starting this direction. Instantly, all my synapses tingle and snap to attention. I'm not going to like where he's going with this, am I?

"Day?"

"Fuck," he spits out the word. "I don't want to tell you this, Rav, but forewarned is forearmed, right?"

I really don't like where this is going. "Spill. What's going on?"

He drops his hands from behind his neck and meets my gaze. "I saw Sasha last night."

Five little words guaranteed to make my head explode.

Only one of those words is needed: Sasha.

That fucking bitch.

In my thirty-two years of life, I've never felt this kind of anger towards a woman, but Sasha has the ability to make those monsters surface. I take a breath and count back from ten, but no amount of counting it out is going to fix this shit.

I had no idea I could become so entwined with one person that she could become my reason for existing. I had no idea how much it would shred me when she was no longer in my life.

"You okay, Prez?" Daimon peers at me and points at my eye. "You've got this twitch thing—"

"Where?" I grind out.

He grimaces. "Oh, man, come on, don't torture yourself."

"Where?" I repeat.

"She was coming out of the hospital on Gillespie. The past is best left where it is."

Usually, I would agree, but Sasha isn't just my past. She's my present, future, and everything in between. Why in the hell is she back in town? When she left, she didn't look back, and I didn't expect to see her again—not on my turf. She's either stupid or brave coming back here. I don't know which, but what I do know is she can't be here when I am.

"Do you need a minute, or ten?" Daimon asks, leaning against the bar.

The patch on the left breast of his kutte reads 'Treasurer', just as mine says 'President'. Yeah, this daft arse is my money man. He's in his early thirties but most of the time acts like he's in his early sixties. I don't care, though, because he makes the pennies and the pounds disappear and reappear in legitimate ways. He keeps all of us out of prison doing it. The leather vest he wears is worn around the neckline and arm holes, but it's not as battered as mine, but then I've got a few years on him. Even so, he's one of my best men.

Right now, though, I want to punch his stupid face in.

"Was she alone?" I grit out.

"Yeah."

I shouldn't ask. I shouldn't care, but I do anyway. "Did she look…"

"She looked fine," he finishes my unspoken question.

My hands go behind my head, my fingers interlocking at my nape. "Fuck. What's she doing here?"

"Do you want me to find out?"

I point at him. "You stay away from her. Everyone stays away from her. That's an order."

"Rav, come on. You can't mean that. I know she did you dirty, but she's Priest's kid—"

"I don't give a fuck. He's dead. She's got no reason to be here anymore. I see anyone talking to her, being around her, I'll kick them out of this clubhouse myself."

I don't wait for his response. I turn and walk away before I say anything else I'm going to regret, but fuck, knowing Sasha is back in town is messing with my head. I head straight for my office, needing to be alone to digest this shit.

Sasha Montgomery.

Fuck me.

That's a name I didn't think I'd hear again. Not ever. Not with how she left. Coming back is ballsy, but then again, she always has been. It is one of the things I love about her—loved about her.

2

SASHA

BEING BACK in Kessington is giving me palpitations, although I don't let any sign of that show on my face. I'll never show my fear. To show fear is a way for people to take advantage, and I had that happen to me once. I'll never repeat it.

Even so, everywhere I look, I'm sure I see bikers or hear the rumbling of pipes, but it's all in my head. I haven't seen any members of the Untamed Sons since I came back to town—a town I thought I'd left behind for good.

It doesn't give me warm or happy memories being here.

The borough of Kessington is no different from any other in London. It's got its share of good and bad people. There are high-rises that line the horizon and most of the high street has moved onto more affluent parts of the city, leaving boarded up shops tagged with graffiti. At some points in the day the smog from the traffic is so bad it's like moving through a fog, so living above the smog is considered prime real estate.

It's also home to the Untamed Sons, a motorcycle club with a reputation so dark, it's said hell spat them back out. They rule Kessington with an ironclad fist. No one operates in the borough without their say so. Those who do disappear fast.

There was a time when this was home. It was all I ever knew and all I ever wanted to know. My life was as entwined with the Sons as Tyler's was. He was always destined to become president, just as I was destined to stand at his side as his old lady. That had been the way we envisaged it from before Ty was old enough to even ride and I was too young to know what being an old lady entailed. Now, I'm twenty-eight and have lived a life most people double my age never have.

But I broke the cardinal rule. I walked away from the president of one of the most notorious MCs in the country and I did it without any hesitation. At the time, I needed to disappear, to leave my life behind. I didn't consider the damage, what the fallout would be. I didn't consider how much my actions would hurt Ty.

Then the fear came, because while I knew the old Tyler would never hurt me, I wasn't so sure about the man who was morphing into 'Ravage'. He was a different beast, one I was still finding my feet with. Now, I'm not sure what he'd do to me if he sees me.

Part of me thinks I deserve whatever he'd dole out. I was, after all, the one who disappeared without any explanation. I was the one who hurt him, but I had my reasons. Good ones, at the time. Now, I'm not so sure.

Especially now.

Pushing through the crowd of people milling on the pavements, I keep my head down, my hair curtaining my face, hoping I won't be recognised. It goes against everything in my body that tells me to hold my chin high and not give a fuck, but there's more at stake here than just me, and all it takes is for one person to see me and feed it back to Ty. At one time, I was as well known in this town as he was, so I'm taking a risk walking around like this, but I don't have a choice. This is the only hospital in the area that could treat Lily-May and for her I'd walk on broken glass or step into the fire.

That doesn't mean I need to bring drama unnecessarily to my door, so I'll avoid it as long as I can.

Being back here brings demons, ones I can't keep at bay. Everywhere I look I see memories of another time, a time that eventually destroyed me. A time that I'm still healing from.

I stomp down on those thoughts, push those monsters aside and ignore the churning in my gut as I step through the hospital's doors. My heart still races, though, a sign of my apprehension.

I'm itching to get Lily-May out of this poisonous place, even though I know she needs to be here. Kessington has the power to seep into even the good things in life and corrode them.

After I left Tyler high and dry, I moved to the other side of London and that's where I met Lucy. When I first left, I got a job in a bar. I wasn't qualified to do anything else. Lucy was working there too and we were both struggling to make rent. When she asked me to share a flat with her, I jumped at the chance. I was about to become a single parent. I didn't have a lot of options. Over the past three years, she's been my rock and has taken care of me and Lily-May better than family. I'll always be grateful for that.

I pass the nurses' station and give the on-duty nurse a wave.

"How's she been?"

"She was a little cranky this morning, but she'll be better for seeing you," Jessa says. I like this nurse. She's been good to me and Lil in the time we've been here. As usual, her hair is pulled up into a ponytail and her cheeks are rosy. "Did you manage to get some sleep?"

"A little." Then I admit, "I just wanted to get back here."

After a solid week at the hospital, I needed to shower and recharge for a few hours. I didn't want to leave, but I needed that time to just get my shit together, so I can be strong for my daughter.

"Understandable, but it is important to take care of yourself, too." There's a hint of chastisement in her words that barely penetrates. I know she means well, but I don't need a lecture. I'm used to being exhausted. I'm used to running on no sleep and not showering for days at a time, because I'm a single mum and that's been my life since Lil was first born.

"So everyone keeps telling me, but while Lily-May is in the hospital, all I care about is her. I'm not even thinking about myself."

"You're a good mum," Jessa tells me and her words, which should make me beam with pride, make my stomach churn with an ugly feeling.

Guilt.

I'm a terrible mother.

I paint a smile on my face and forge past the nurses' station and into the room that has become my life for almost seven days now.

The sterile smell of the cleaning fluids mixes with the scent of sweat and illness that clings to the air. The machines at the side of the bed beep in a steady rhythmic tone that grates on my nerves every time I hear it, because it reminds me of my truth—that things are no longer okay.

Lucy glances up from the magazine she's flicking through and gives me a smile that's filled with warmth. I would never have survived the past few years without her. She's been the best friend I could never live without and she loves Lily-May as much as I do.

She looks tired, too. Her eyes are surrounded by black circles that mar her pale skin and the freckles on her face seem more pronounced.

My eyes slide to the cot bed and my feet move of their own accord to the side of it before my hand comes to rest on my daughter's belly. She's wearing pyjamas with little motorcycles on them. I might be out of the life, but it hasn't totally let go of its hold on me. I'm still a biker brat at heart. Besides, her jammies are adorable—at least they would be if they didn't have a whole host of wires and tubes snaking out from under the material.

Lily-May's eyes are closed, but flutter a little at my touch, and the urge to play with her beautiful blonde curls is overwhelming, but I don't want to wake her.

"How's she been?" I ask Lucy, keeping my voice soft.

"A little fussy," she says, confirming what the nurse told me, "but she settled eventually and slept probably more than you have, by the look of you."

I watch as she lets her white blonde hair free and redoes it in another sloppy knot.

Lucy is a beautiful person, both inside and out. She was mine and Lily-May's saviour after I left town and she continues to be my saviour now, helping me navigate this nightmare.

"Is she any worse?"

She shakes her head. "About the same really. They gave her some meds an hour ago and she's slept since."

My heart breaks. No parent should have to see their child sick, but this feels like punishment for what I did in the past, for the way I lived my life. I wish the universe would take it out on me, though, not my daughter. In all of this, she is the only innocent one.

"You should go and get some rest," I tell her, but she shakes her head.

"I'm fine, honey. I can stay for a bit."

I don't argue with her. It would be pointless to try when her mind is made up.

Lucy considers me a moment. "How are you doing with everything else? Being back here can't be easy."

Inwardly, I flinch at her perceptiveness. Being back here is hell.

"It's the only hospital in London with a children's department capable of giving Lily-May the treatment she needs," I say instead.

She clucks her tongue at me, letting her frustration show. She's one of the few people who can get away with giving me shit like that, because Lucy is closer than family.

"I didn't ask that, Sasha. I asked how you're doing."

I glance up from my daughter and meet her gaze. My heart is starting to race a little and my palms feel warm. I don't want to talk about how I'm doing. I don't want to relive the nightmare I survived, just barely. All I want is to see to my kid.

"I'm dealing."

Because I have to.

The alternative is my daughter doesn't get her treatment and she dies. That isn't going to happen.

I'm saved from further probing by the doctor entering. Dr Harking has been a godsend, helping Lily-May when the other doctors couldn't. He's the leading cancer specialist in the country, and knows everything there is to know about paediatric cases. When Lily-May took a turn this time, we were transferred over here—to a hospital within the boundaries of the Sons' territory. That was not a good thing for me, but it's the best for my daughter, so the transfer happened. Only the best will do for her.

Still, it's a bitter pill to swallow.

"Did the results come back?" I press, not caring about

making small talk. I want to know if my daughter can be saved, if me or Lucy hold the key to saving her.

My stomach fills with ice as his mouth pulls into a tight line and I know it's going to be bad news. Chills run up my spine as the bottom prepares to drop out of my world.

"It did. I'm sorry, but you're not a full match and Miss Franklin only has one marker in common."

My heart sinks and terror like I've never felt claws at my cardiac muscle. She needs eight to match. That means Lucy can't donate bone marrow. I can, but there are risks with it being only a partial match.

It's a crushing blow and I feel as if I've been sucker punched in the gut. The only chance Lily-May has of surviving this is with a transplant.

Helplessness spreads through me and it's not a feeling I'm used to. My entire life, I've always got by on the seat of my pants. I've always fudged my way through somehow, but there's no fudging this. This is the end of the line. It means Lily-May's chances of survival are diminished significantly. Our only other choice is to transplant from me and risk infection or the transplant not taking, or get her on the national donor register and find an anonymous match, which is going to be tough.

How do I fix the unfixable?

I stagger over to the other chair at the side of the bed and drop into it, my legs feeling unsteady. This is a death knell for her.

"As I told you before the test—immediate family is the best option for a full match, although that's not guaranteed. A sibling gives a higher chance, but Lily-May is an only child, right?"

"Right," I murmur back. Numbness is spreading through me. I feel sick.

"We can put her on the national register and see if we hit a full match on there, but that's all we can do for now."

All we can do…

His words sound like giving up and I'm not ready to lie down and lose my child. Not yet. Not while I'm still breathing.

"What about a parent?" I demand.

His brow draws together. "We already tested you—"

"I'm not talking about me. I'm talking about Lily-May's father. What if I can get him tested?"

"Sash!" Lucy gasps. "You can't."

She knows why I can't. She knows the hurt in my past that made me walk away from my entire life. She also knows doing this will shatter me.

Doing nothing isn't an option, though.

My child needs me, and I'll do whatever it takes to fix this for her—even if it means facing my demons. Even if it means facing a man who all but destroyed me—would have done if it wasn't for my daughter.

I ignore my best friend. It would hurt to do it, to walk into that clubhouse and demand it, but for my daughter, I would suffer anything. When life got dark, she was the only light in my world. She kept me sane, whole and putting one foot in front of the other. I won't lose her because I'm afraid. I'll fight to my last breath for her—even if it means putting myself in the firing line.

The doctor considers it.

"It might help. A father could match more closely than you have, although the chances are still not overly high, but if you can get them here we can do the test."

"I'll get him here," I promise.

I just have to work out which man I'm bringing—Tyler or his brother, James.

3

SASHA

My HEART IS GALLOPING in my chest as I approach the Untamed Sons compound, but something comes over me as it comes into view. My back straightens, and my lips pull into a snarl as I stride towards the gate.

I'm doing this for Lily-May, and that has me putting one foot in front of the other and moving nearer to the entrance of the compound. It has me pushing all my fears aside because for her I can and I will be strong.

The clubhouse sits at the bottom end of a cul-de-sac, behind a wire fence that spans the perimeter. Behind me, the hustle and bustle of London traffic becomes a dull moan as I move further from the main road. Civilisation is just a stone's throw away, but it might as well be a mile. This is the Sons' domain and even if it wasn't for the huge sign over the doors of the compound declaring that, it's written in every stone of the road.

I peer through the chain-link fence at the building I once considered my home. Growing up, I spent a lot of time here. Priest, my father, was always at the clubhouse, so I was here as often as I was allowed. Growing up it was just the two of us. Mum didn't stick around long. Then later, after we started dating, Tyler would bring me. By the time he got made president, I was already deeply embedded in this life. I lived and breathed the Sons, loved the brothers and saw them as family. Losing them was almost as hard as losing Ty.

As I let my eyes roam over the clubhouse, I'm surprised by how little the building has changed in the years I've been gone. It doesn't look any different from the last time I was here, except maybe a little more downtrodden. Ty clearly hasn't kept up with the housekeeping—something I would have made him do.

The squat structure, which spans one floor, looks more like a commercial unit than the headquarters of a notorious biker club. On the outside of the fence line there are bays for parking, which are filled with Harleys that make my stomach flip with a hint of excitement. I always loved being on the back of Rav's bike. I loved wrapping my arms around his waist and hitting the open road, just me and him. It's been too long since I last rode.

My eyes trail to the other side of the gate and the rows of bikes beyond it. The chrome glints in the mid-afternoon sunlight, creating a sea of sparkling lights that line the road to the gate like an airport landing strip. It's kind of beautiful, which seems at odds with the hardness of the rest of the surroundings.

As I reach the gate, I pause. There's no bell, no way of letting anyone know I'm here. That's because coming to the clubhouse is invite only, and I doubt I'm on that list. Knowing these men as I do, they already know I'm here. They probably knew the moment I turned into the street.

"Are you lost, sweetheart?" a young guy with dark hair asks, stepping out of a small booth at the side of the gate. He looks maybe eighteen or nineteen, but his swagger tells me he's been with the Sons for a little while. His gaze rakes over me in a way that would have most women squirming, but I grew up in this life. I'm more than used to the men that live in it, and I know how to handle them.

"Do I look lost?" I raise my eyebrow, holding his eyes. I don't flatter him like the club pussy would and I see as he narrows his eyes that it unnerves him. A smirk plays across my lips. "I'm looking for Ravage."

I decide to start with the lesser of two evils. Facing Rav will be easier than facing Sin. I'm not sure I have the strength to see him yet, but I will. For Lily-May, I'll talk to him.

The prospect's demeanour changes from playful to on guard in an instant. I see the moment the steel shutters come down and I don't blame him. It would make anyone in the club edgy if some bitch showed up asking to see their president—especially when that bitch looks like me.

I may have left the biker life behind, but it hasn't completely left me. I have short black hair that is so dark it looks dyed, but it's my natural colour. It reaches just past my chin, following the line of my jaw. The leather jacket I'm wearing is beat around the edges, scuffed and marked up from years of use. Beneath the sleeve, it's just possible to see the tattoo on my wrist of my daughter's name in a heart. On my other I wear a heap of silver and black bangles. Dark eyeshadow and eyeliner rim my eyes, making them look hard.

The prospect glares at me like I'm a live bomb. "And you are?"

"Aren't you a good boy, asking all the right questions?"

I don't see any patches on his kutte and judging from how new the leather looks, I'm guessing he's a prospect or he's relatively newly patched in because I don't recognise him either. He's definitely not from my generation of bikers.

This might make things easier. The others hate my guts.

"Sasha." I don't give him any more than my name. I don't need to.

When he twists slightly to look in the direction of the clubhouse, I glimpse the back of his kutte, the leather vest all bikers wear, and I see the word 'Prospect'.

I was right then. This guy is green as grass.

I trail a finger over the chain-link fence and sadness comes over me. It feels weird to be this side of the fence and not a good weird. I didn't realise how much I've missed this place until now—even with the bad memories. There was a lot of good that happened here too.

"Don't move," the prospect warns, and I put my hands up in mock-surrender, rolling my eyes.

This gets me a glare as he pulls his phone out and dials before holding it to his ear. I don't blame his suspicion. He doesn't know me from Adam. Ironically, only a few short years ago keeping me out here would have cost this guy his kutte. How much things have changed because of one mistake I made—because I trusted the wrong man.

I swallow that down and slide my eyes in the direction of the clubhouse hoping, praying, that I don't run into Sin. I don't know that I'm strong enough to deal with seeing him yet, although I'll need to get strong enough. I need that sample. I need to know if he's a match for Lily-May. Nothing else matters right now. Not the past, not the future, not a damned thing.

Even so, I steel myself for the coming storm.

It comes sooner than anticipated.

"Bitch, you're not welcome here," a familiar voice declares, venom behind the words.

Nox.

Of all the brothers, I always liked him best. He was the most laid-back of the bunch, even with a body filled with artwork and an attitude that could rival a rattlesnake. He was always kind to me, but I hurt his president and these men are nothing if not loyal to each other. I'll be lucky if he doesn't gut me on the spot.

"Nox." I sound bored and school my features before taking a look at him. This man could end me with a word and I'd disappear into the ether, never to be found again. The Sons are good at making things vanish.

What I get back from him is suspicion and outright hostility.

He shakes his head. "Ain't happening."

"Nox—"

"No chance, you ain't seeing him, and if you've got any sense in that head of yours, you'll get the fuck out of town before he sees you."

I figured this might be his answer, but I'm not deterred. Fear for Lily-May makes me bolder than I might have been under other circumstances.

"Do you think I'd be here if I had a fucking choice?" I spit back at him, the anger of the past three years overtaking everything else.

Nox glares at me. It's a look that would intimidate even the evillest of people, but I grew up in this world, around these men. I knew Nox from when we were little kids. I'm not scared of him.

Although Nox the boy is different from Nox the man.

Worlds apart.

He's always been a big lad, even when we were teens he was pushing six foot. Now, he's maybe six-three, around thirty-years-old, if memory serves, and has a thin layer of hair covering his head. His eyes, which used to be filled with life, are too shrewd, too hard. He looks like a man who has seen shit and done shit he can never take back. Probably, that's true. I have no illusions that these men are Boy Scouts.

This Nox looks like he's contemplating putting a bullet in

21

my brain. I feel a tendril of fear work up my spine, even as I keep my external expression neutral.

"You've got some fucking nerve coming here, Sash."

"Yeah," I mutter, "that's me. A ballsy bitch. Are you getting Rav or not?"

"Not."

My eyes slide to the prospect who is finishing up the call. He shifts on his feet and then says a little hesitantly, "Uh, Rav's on his way. Sin's coming too."

Ice fills my veins and my guard must momentarily lower, because Nox's lip twitches as he raises his brow. He thinks it's Rav that caused my reaction, but it's not him who makes my skin crawl. It's Sin.

My lips curl up into a snarl like I'm a trapped animal ready to come out and fight. I have to push my disgust down. I'm not here to put old demons to rest. I'm here for my daughter.

Nox glares at me, his big arms folding over his chest, rucking his kutte up. Unlike the prospect's, his is filled with patches—including the one percent badge and the number thirteen.

I resist the urge to fidget as we wait. I don't want to show any sign I'm on edge, even though I am. It's hard to keep still with Nox's eyes boring into my head like sharpened daggers, though.

"Why'd you come back, Sash?" he asks finally. "You have to know Rav's going to lose his mind seeing you again."

I open my mouth to answer, but the sound of a door slamming has my eyes straying past Nox and the prospect towards the main clubhouse. For the first time in three years, I get a look at the man who was once my everything.

My heart clenches painfully.

His dark hair is pulled into a tie at the nape of his neck and the thick beard covering his chin is a new addition. He usually wore a little scruff when we were together. This makes him seem harder. The leather kutte he's wearing is as beat up as my jacket and moulded to his body like a second skin, covered in patches. Beneath it he has on a dark shirt and a pair of jeans that should be illegal, they're so well fitted. My gaze trails up his sharp jaw, and come to rest on his eyes, which are colder than a glacier.

I swallow hard and my heart starts to pound.

Then I see Sin and my world stops. He looks like his brother, sans the beard and his eyes are not hard, but amused, as if he doesn't have a care in the world. I hate him for that more than anything. I hate that he ruined my life and thinks this is a big joke.

Lily-May's face dances in my consciousness, and it gives me the strength to face the man who may or may not be her father. It gives me the strength to stand in front of a man I've killed a thousand times in my dreams.

"What the fuck are you doing here, Sasha?" Tyler's angry voice demands.

No, not Tyler, but Ravage. Tyler would never have spoken to me like that.

I have to remember the two men are not the same, and I am responsible for the man in front of me. I created Ravage when I left. I cemented the man he is now.

"I need to talk. Alone." I eye Nox and Sin. I notice the prospect has made himself scarce. It's probably a good idea. Prospects tend to be on the firing line when rage is going around.

And this is going to get messy.

"Why don't you drag your arse off my property before I do something we'll both regret."

He's barely keeping a rein on his temper, his fists clenching and unclenching at his sides, as if it's taking all his power to control his emotions. I don't blame his anger, even if I'm not sure it's justified. I had my reasons for leaving and if I had to do it again, I'd still leave because I needed that space between me, Rav and Sin.

I close my eyes, letting the first emotion slip through. When I reopen them, I see Sin is grinning at me.

I glance between the two men. Then I drop the bombshell.

"One of you has a daughter, and I need your help."

Sin's no longer grinning.

Rav's expression is darker than a full-blown storm.

The next thing I know, I'm looking down the barrel of a gun. Fear dances across my skin, but I hold firm, my chin high, as I meet Rav's gaze unflinchingly.

"My daughter," I emphasise the 'my', letting them know who she belongs to, that she is nothing to them, "has leukaemia. She's dying. She needs a bone marrow transplant like yesterday. There's an appointment booked tomorrow at ten-thirty a.m. at Kessington General Hospital in the children's department to see if one of you is a match." I pull a photograph from my wallet of her three months ago and hold it against the fence. She's smiling, her red toddler cheeks blown out as she laughs at something. Her blonde hair makes her look angelic. She's also in a hospital bed, which is where she's spent most of the last few months.

Rav's arm shakes, his finger sliding on the trigger. I don't cower, instead, I take a step back. I know he won't shoot me. At least the old Rav wouldn't have.

"Be there, or I'll come back." I let the threat hang in the air between the men, my expression telling them how serious I am.

"Move again and I'll fucking shoot," Rav warns, but I ignore him.

I hope that I still know these men, that no matter how much blood covers their hands, how many people they've made disappear, I hope they still hold to the fact they don't hurt women—not without a solid reason.

"Deceitful whore," Rav hisses at me. I don't even flinch at his words, although they have the power to wound like bullets to the chest. Three years ago they might have.

I let my eyes slide to Sin, letting my disgust for the man pour out of me. I don't miss Nox watching us, his shrewd eyes intent. Let him think what he wants. I don't care.

When I bring my gaze back to Rav, I repeat, "Be there tomorrow."

"We're not done here," he growls at me. "Fucking explain this."

"You come tomorrow and I'll tell you everything." I glare at Sin then I stare at Rav a beat. Then I do what I did three years ago. I turn my back on him and on the club.

4

RAVAGE

I FEEL my knuckles crack as the next punch lands. Sin doesn't beg me to stop, doesn't say a word, but takes his beating like a good little cunt. The rage flaring through me is so electric, so heavy, I can't stop it. I want to kill him—brother or not—for taking something that belonged to me, for throwing loyalty aside and shitting all over it.

After Sasha left the compound, I dragged him into the clubhouse and let my temper unleash. He's lucky I didn't put a bullet straight between his eyes, although I still might.

I've gathered an audience, no doubt all wondering why their president has gone off the deep end and is beating the shit out of his kid brother, but no one moves to intervene, no one asks why I'm suddenly giving Sin a beat down either.

This is the way of our world. My word is law and if I'm hitting him there's a good reason.

And this time there's a very good reason.

He and Sasha betrayed me and Sin is getting the brunt of the anger raging through me like a speeding train. The urge to pull the trigger on her had been a battle too, but no matter how much she's destroyed me, I can't play tit-for-tat with her.

I level a punch at my brother's stomach, relishing the grunt he makes in response. Sin is already a bloodied mess—so am I. He strikes my jaw with enough force to snap my head back and I retaliate with another uppercut to the gut that nearly takes him off his feet.

No one touches what's mine.

He doesn't get a pass because he's family.

"She ain't exactly innocent in this, Rav," he says through mushy lips. "I was drunk off my head. I didn't know what day of the week it was."

The idea of Sasha taking advantage of him is laughable, but doubt clings at his words—doubt I don't want to feel. Did she do this? Who do I believe? Her or him?

"You still fell into bed with her," I growl, circling him, my fists ready. Blood is spurting down the side of my face, soaking the collar of my kutte.

"It was dark. How the fuck was I meant to know! I wish it never fucking happened. I wish I could undo it. I didn't tell you because I knew you'd take her side."

I laugh at his words even as uncertainty attacks my mind. My fist flashes out, catching him in the side of the head as his reflexes slow.

He absorbs the blow, weaving on his feet a little. "These bitches just want one thing. They're all kutte sluts. She thought she could have the Prez and the VP eating out of her fucking palm."

His words eviscerate me. It doesn't match with the Sasha I know, but the evidence doesn't suggest it could be otherwise.

Whether he seduced her or she took advantage of him, the outcome was still the same. Them fucking, her having a kid she can't put a father to.

27

I seize the lapels of Sin's kutte, dragging him closer. He hangs in my grip like a rag doll, his eyes rolling in his head. Without remorse, I pull my fist back and slam it into his face again. My brother grins dazedly at me through bloodied teeth and I want to wipe that fucking smirk off his face. I want to wrap my fingers around his scrawny neck for daring to touch her—even though I shouldn't care.

It's been three years since Sasha left me.

Three years and yet that bitch can still elicit a nuclear level of anger from me.

I hate her for that. I don't want to feel anything for her, but knowing she fucked my brother before she left makes my temper boil over. Knowing she might have a kid with him makes me positively homicidal.

She's the only woman I've ever let in and her betrayal cuts like a thousand knives.

Sin's hardly moving now, and as I go in for another shot, Nox wraps an arm around my throat and pulls me back. I fight him. Hell, I'll fight any fucker in this room right now, but his grip on my neck is like a vice. It's enough to stop me in my tracks.

"He's had enough, Prez," he hisses in my ear.

"He's had enough when I say he's had enough," I growl, bucking against the hold on me.

Nox is a big guy, but I'm bigger. Right now, though, he has a solid hold, and he's not letting go, and my reflexes are slowed by the return beating I took from Sin.

"You're going to kill him."

He says that like it's not my intention.

"I don't care."

I try to pull away from him, but Daimon gets the other side of me, and together both men manage to drag me back. Frustration roars through me and I pull out of their grasps, shoving the guy who happens to be nearest—Daimon—as my breath saws out of me.

I glance at the lump of meat on the floor behind them, my lips curled into a snarl.

Sin lies still, staring up at the ceiling with glassy eyes, blood covering every inch of his face. His breath sounds wet when he inhales and I'm sure I've done internal damage somewhere. I don't give a fuck about that.

"You touched something that belongs to me!" I roar in his direction.

Day and Nox stand between me and him, stopping me from inflicting any more damage.

I should care that I'm doing this with an audience, but it might do the peanut gallery a favour to see what happens if you cross me.

"Was drunk... she came... on to me." He repeats his shit story and coughs, a rasping wet sound as blood bubbles on his lips.

Pain slices through my chest.

"I don't fucking believe you."

"She left... 'cause I... I threatened... to tell you."

His words gore me. Deceitful bastards, the pair of them.

"Had no idea... it was her until after. It was dark, man... couldn't see."

I want to believe that. I want to believe it so badly. I don't want to think my own brother could betray me like this, but I smell the shit coming off his words. Everything he says is a lie and doubts are creeping in over what else the fucker has lied to me about over the years.

"Get him out of my fucking sight," I growl to no one in particular.

Whizz, our resident doctor, moves towards him, crouching at his side. I shake my head.

"No fucking pain meds, Whizz. I want that fucker to feel

every bruise I gave him." I lean around Daimon as Titch helps Whizz to pull Sin up. "We ain't done here, little brother. Not even close."

I storm from the room, passing Fury who is leaning against the wall, watching with a blank look on his face.

As I step into the corridor, I put my fist through the dry wall before I tear into my office like a man possessed. I clear the desk with one sweeping motion of my arm, the papers going flying. It doesn't make me feel better.

Sinking into my desk chair, I reach for the Scotch I keep in my drawer, ignoring my torn-up knuckles. I don't bother with a glass, I drink straight from the bottle, relishing the burn as it hits my throat.

My blood is boiling as I think about her with Sin, as I think about him taking something he shouldn't have touched.

My head feels like it might explode.

She fucked my brother—a brother who has stood at my side as my vice president since she left.

A brother I all but raised and took care of better than myself over the years.

I don't know who I'm more pissed at—her or him.

My thoughts calm slightly when I think about the little kid in the photograph Sasha showed me. She could be my daughter. She looks like me, but she looks like Sin, too.

If this kid is mine, I'm furious that Sasha hid her from me, that she stopped me from knowing my daughter.

If she's not mine…

I tear a hand through my hair which has come loose from the tie and slug back another swig of Scotch.

I hear a noise and I don't need to look up to know who is in my doorway. I should have expected it, because Nox is as predictable as the day is long.

"You level, brother?" he asks.

It's a redundant question because he can clearly see I'm not even close to level. I'm covered in blood, mostly Sin's, though some of it is my own. My little brother did land some good punches.

"Shut the fucking door on your way out," I order, using the bottle to gesture in that direction. I'm not in the mood for a chit-chat right now.

He doesn't do as I demand, but instead steps further into the room. Bolshy bastard. He's the only man in this club that would get away with defying a direct order and only because I've known Nox most of my life. He knows me better than anyone, even my own brother—especially now.

"Sin's a dirty bastard."

I snort as a thousand betrayals stab at my gut. He's not telling me something I don't know.

"If you want me to keep wrecking shit, keep talking about that fucker."

He runs a hand over his jaw, which is covered in a layer of scruff and I can see the cogs in his head working on overdrive. Nox has always been a thinker. I should have made him my VP, not Sin, but I chose loyalty to family over loyalty to a man who actually deserved it.

"Something about this situation stinks, Rav."

My gaze snaps to his face and I let my disbelief play over my face. "No shit."

Nox leans against the wall, his head slightly bowed and I can see he's trying to figure this out in his brain. He's a problem solver and right now he sees this as a problem, instead of seeing it for what it really is—my little brother's inability to keep his dick in his jeans.

"Sash… she didn't seem exactly happy about seeing your brother. There's no love lost there."

I grit my teeth and lean back in my seat, my rage flaring again that he'd take her side in this.

"Jesus fucking Christ, are you eating that bitch's pussy too? Because it sure as fuck sounds like you're sticking up for a whore here."

The words are said with anger and designed to wound, designed to get some of my own rage out.

I'm not surprised when he riles at this. "Fuck you, Rav. I would never go there with your woman and you know that."

He wouldn't and I should feel bad for suggesting it, but all I feel right now is fury that not even the Scotch is dulling.

"I know Sin's lying," I tell him, my voice a little less harsh. "I'm not a fucking idiot."

His story sounds like something a fucking child would tell and I know my brother. I know all his ticks and tells. He's lying his arse off. He knew exactly what he was doing and who with. He just didn't give a fuck.

"Sasha… she didn't seem right," Nox presses.

"She fucked him and might have a kid with him. Ain't nothing right here."

The words are like ash in my mouth and saying them makes my stomach churn with bile. Rage starts to build again in my gut.

"She seemed… disgusted by him. Does that sound like someone who seduced a man in the dark and took advantage while he was drunk?"

It doesn't, but I never thought Sash was a devious, deceitful bitch either. Now, I know different.

"I don't know what the fuck to believe. I don't even care. They both fucked me over."

Nox weighs me with his stare.

"I've never known Sash to be anything but loyal. This ain't like her."

I snort at this suggestion even as doubts assail me. Nox doesn't have a horse in this race. He has no reason to side with either of them.

I'm still seething, so I can't stop my angry retort. "She's no better than a club bunny."

Nox rolls his eyes at my words. "You know that ain't true."

"Do I? My woman left because she was knocked up by my brother. How's that any different from those bitches wanting to get their claws into any brother with a patch?"

"Sash was one of us once. Try to remember that." He stares at me a beat, then says, "Just think on it, okay? I'll have a prospect bring another bottle of Scotch."

He bangs his fist off the wall lightly and strides from my office, leaving me with my turbulent thoughts.

5

SASHA

Rav and Sin don't show up the next morning. I didn't expect they would after I dropped the ticking time bomb that one of them is a father, but I hoped. Foolishly, stupidly, I hoped they would put the past aside and do this to save a little girl's life.

Anger surges through my veins that they were incapable of letting go of our shit for just five seconds, but it's followed by a feeling of helplessness. They're Lily-May's last hope. She needs this.

They might not even be a match, filters across my brain and I hate that it does. I don't need to be thinking negative thoughts right now. Only positive. My baby is going to survive this. She's going to get that transplant and be right as rain again.

It's the only hope I have to cling to as I pace the hospital corridor, glancing up at the clock.

I nibble on my bottom lip.

Eleven-thirty.

They're an hour late.

A sinking feeling is hitting the pit of my stomach, one that tells me this isn't going the way I want.

"I don't think they're coming, honey," Lucy tells me, her voice soft, as if that can lessen the blow.

It doesn't.

"We just need to give them a little longer." I sound desperate. I know time won't make a lick of difference, but I have to hold on to that. I have to believe neither men hate me so much they'd let a baby die.

I look at the clock again, watching the time tick down.

They're not coming.

I expected it from Sin. That bastard wouldn't lift a finger to help me before, but I thought he might feel a hint of remorse that might guilt him into coming. Rav... Knowing him as I do, I'm guessing he lost his shit over what I told him and has spent the last few hours buried in a bottle of Scotch.

I snag my jacket from the chair and shrug into it.

"Where are you going?" Lucy asks, coming to her feet with me.

"Back to the clubhouse."

"Sash, you can't. Ravage pointed a gun at your head last time you were there. What do you think he'll do to you now he's had time to think about all of this?"

Probably put a bullet in me, but if I can get him to the hospital before he does that...

"They're Lily-May's last hope."

"The national register—"

"Won't save her. The chances of finding a match are slim to none. A full match is her best shot. Rav or Sin could be that."

"I hope you know what you're doing." Her voice tells me she doesn't think I'm doing the right thing, but I love her for not trying to talk me out of this crazy plan. She knows I'll do anything for my daughter, even walk back through the fires of hell.

I fix my jacket in place and grab my bag.

"If they do turn up, call me."

She comes to her feet and pulls me into a hug. "Please be careful, honey. Lily-May needs her mother alive and kicking, not buried in some MC's backyard."

"They won't hurt me," I assure her, hoping that's true. They never used to harm women, but a lot has changed over the past few years, including Rav. I don't know what these men stand for any longer, but I hope it's the same as it was in the past.

Rav's different now, harder, although he always was—just not with me. I can't blame him for reacting the way he has. I dropped a grenade and walked away, but I had to. Being in his and Sin's presence is too difficult. It brings back too many memories of a time I'd rather forget. I don't think I've been happy one day since I left. Other than Lil. She's the sunshine in my cloudy sky, and I'll never feel anything but joy at having her—no matter how she came into this world.

Because she's mine. *Mine*. And I'll fight for her to my dying breath, which may come sooner rather than later, if Rav is feeling less than benevolent.

It's a bit of a walk to the clubhouse, but it's warm today, so I go on foot. Besides, I need the time to think. Nerves jangle through me, but my mind is focused on getting the help I need for my daughter—even if it backfires on me. I'll take whatever punishment is offered, so long as they agree to help her.

As I approach the gates of the clubhouse, I lift my chin higher and exude an air of calm I absolutely do not feel. Inside, I'm a trembling wreck. I need to get this for Lily-May and nothing will stand in my way. Not Rav, not Sin —nothing.

I stand in front of the gates and after a moment the same prospect from yesterday appears from the hut at the side.

He eyes me warily, but he doesn't say a word to me. Instead, he gets straight on the phone.

I wait, my patience wearing thin as I prowl the fence line like a wildcat.

I expect to see Rav appear from the clubhouse, but it's Nox.

Great.

Getting past the gatekeeper isn't going to be easy.

He doesn't bother with hello as he nears me. "Get fucking gone, now."

I steel my jaw, and slip my fingers through the chain-link fence that separates us. "I told him I'd be back if no one showed to the appointment. Big surprise, no one showed, so here I am."

He snorts at me. "You've got a fucking death wish."

"I just want help for my daughter, Nox. I get that and I'll disappear again. Poof, like I never existed."

The way he's looking at me, I guess he's wishing that I'd do that anyway. He's probably thinking about how he can make that happen.

"Rav isn't going to help you, and Sin's in no condition to do shit right now."

His words take a moment to sink in and when they do, I can't help but smirk. I'm guessing him and Rav got into it last night. I can't say I feel any remorse that Sin obviously took a beating.

Nox's face pulls into a snarl. "You think this shit is funny? Pitting brother against brother?"

"I think Sin got exactly what he deserves."

He deserves so much worse.

He tilts his head to one side, considering me like I'm a puzzle. "What's going on there, Sash? Did something happen between you and Sin?"

I roll my eyes. "Do I need to teach you about the birds and the bees, Nox?"

This makes him chuckle, but there's no humour in it. "I'm not talking about you both getting your rocks off. I'm talking about the fact you seem a little pissed at the guy."

I could answer. I could spill everything right now, but he'd never believe me. No one will. Sin told me that at the time. It's the only truth he spilled that night and it's the only truth I've been sure of over the past three years—that I wouldn't be believed. I'm not big on trying to prove myself.

Instead, I hedge with, "You'd have to ask him."

"I'm asking you."

I eye him, my mouth twisting up at the corners.

"I'm not here to rehash the past, Nox. I'm here for my kid. Where's Rav and Sin?"

"Not coming."

I try a different tact, realising I'm never going to get through the wall he's built between us.

"She's a baby. She needs help." I'm not above begging, if it gets me what I want. I'll appeal to whatever side of Nox I have to. He's not swayed though.

"You fucked around on Rav. You think he's going to give a shit about helping you?"

I sigh at his outburst. "I'd prefer to hear that from his mouth."

"Then hear it from my mouth," Rav's voice breaks through the tension. I glance to the side and see him crossing the tarmac towards us. "I don't give a shit about helping you."

When he reaches the gate, he looks me over like I'm shit under his boots.

I lift my chin a little higher and take a moment to study the man who was once my world. Now, I'm not sure what he is. Old feelings still sit on the precipice. One hard push would shove them over.

My eyes rake over Rav's face and I feel a hint of satisfaction as I take in his injuries. Judging from the cut over his brow and the layers of bruises down his jaw, he and Sin got into it pretty bad after I left. I hope Sin came worse off. He deserves everything he gets. I just wish Rav hadn't got caught up in it.

But I'm not here to see justice get dished out. I'm here for Lily-May.

"Rav—"

He moves up to the fence and hisses at me, "You're lucky I don't put a bullet in you right now."

"I know you think I'd deserve that, but I don't. I didn't do anything wrong."

"You fucked my brother," he counters, "and got pregnant."

Pain lances through my chest at his words, pain that steals my breath. "That's the past. I don't care about that. All I care about is my daughter. You never showed."

"Did I say I was going to?"

"Are you really going to do nothing? She could be yours, and even if she's not, she's your niece. I thought family was important to you."

I throw that back in his face, because Rav has always been about family—whether that's blood or club.

"You don't know shit about me."

"I used to know more than anyone."

I see a thin break in the wall, but only because I can still read Rav. He keeps it locked tightly behind titanium walls.

"Get the fuck off my property before I do something we both regret."

I give him a defiant glare. "Not until you promise to help my daughter."

"I ain't promising shit to you. You fucked me over, bitch."

His words cut me, but I ignore the dirty feeling that washes over me. "Are you helping or not?"

"Not."

"Then I guess I'll be back tomorrow."

I turn, walking away, but stop at the sound of the gate opening. Rav starts towards me and the look in his eyes should scare me but it doesn't. I don't fear Rav, although I probably should. I've known him since we were kids, and the man has been inside me more times than I can count.

"I mean it, Sash. Don't come back here."

"Then do the test."

"Is she mine or Sin's?"

I swallow back the years of pain that question brings up. "I don't know."

His jaw tightens and I see the ripple of disgust that goes through him. It's nothing compared to the things I've said to myself over the years, the uncleanness I felt seeing Sin again after all this time. "If you won't do this for me, Rav, do it for my father."

Anger contorts his face.

"That's low, bringing Priest into this."

I shrug. "I'll bring anyone into this if I think it'll get my daughter the help she needs."

He scowls at me, then hisses out, "What time tomorrow?"

"Ten."

"I'll be there. Then, we're fucking talking about this."

Relief floods me. It's followed quickly by a hint of anger.

"Yeah, Rav, we'll do that. Show up this time," I tell him. Then I walk away from the compound and the man I once professed to love—a man I still love.

6

RAVAGE

"Do you need help relaxing tonight, Rav?" Melody's voice would usually have me hard as a rock, but right now it's grating on my nerves.

She flips her red hair over her shoulders and pushes her fake tits out at me, a move that would usually get my attention. I don't even glance at them, which tells me all I need to know.

My mind is elsewhere.

Melody's been with the club for a couple of years now, working her way through my boys like a knife through hot butter. She has a mouth like a hoover, which is the only reason I indulge her. Tonight, I'm not in the mood for club bunnies or anything else, though.

Tonight, my mind is full of a certain dark-haired Sasha.

I lean my forearms heavily on the bar and roll my tumbler of Scotch between my fingers.

Even thinking her name has my stomach twisting. Facing her tomorrow will be a coin flip as to whether I lose my shit or not.

I want answers to what the hell is going on, and I hope

like fuck she gives them to me. I'm tired of being led around by her.

I want to know if Nox is right. He seems to think there's more going on than I'm seeing, but I'm not convinced. It seems pretty cut and shut to me. She cheated and left.

Once, Sasha was the reason I existed. She was my world and kept all the darkness, all the demons that dog my steps at bay just long enough to make it through each day. Then she became the reason those demons were unleashed. Like Fury, once I was out of the box, there was no going back in it. I'm a different man now than the one she left behind. There's no changing that. I'm scarred by the past.

Daimon slides onto the bar stool next to me as Melody sashays off to find another victim. I watch her go before returning my gaze to my Scotch.

He puts a hand up for a drink, which Kyle brings to him, sliding it in front of him like a good little prospect should.

"It's done," is all he says as he takes a sip of his pint.

He doesn't need to explain. I know he's talking about the money we laundered through our legal businesses. We had a big windfall from some of our drug running this week and it needed to disappear in ways we can spend it. As my money man, that falls to Daimon.

I don't say anything, just sip my drink, letting the amber liquid burn my gullet as it goes down. I relish it. I need it. Feeling something is better than feeling nothing. Except my problem right now is I feel too much and I hate it. All my old wounds are torn open for the world to see—because of her.

I don't know how to bring my walls down again, so I'm drinking myself into oblivion.

I don't want to see her tomorrow, but I said I would be at the hospital and I'm a man of my word, so I'll be there. I want answers. I want to know why she fucked my brother when I thought things between us were good.

I haven't seen Sin since I beat several shades of hell out of him. I have no idea what condition he's in. I don't care either. The urge to strip him of his colours is chipping away at my every thought. I don't know why I haven't yet—the club bylaws would allow it—but something, some gut feeling, tells me I need to see this unfold, and if there's one thing I trust, it's my gut.

"Everything is on track for the run tomorrow?" I ask him. We have a drop off to do. Half a million pounds worth of cocaine to move to our supplier, Dizzy—a wannabe gangster who distributes our product. It's risky, but it's a run the boys do every other week, so they're used to taking the necessary precautions to keep them off the law's radar. Even if they get on that radar, I have a lot of the local plod on the payroll.

"Titch has the route planned. Me and Levi are going with him."

"Take the prospect too." I glance up at Kyle who is stocking the bar. The kid works hard, and he's shown himself as dependable.

He nods, taking my orders without question.

I bang my knuckles on the bar, telling Daimon I'm done, and push up from the stool. I don't want company tonight, so I walk through the common room, ignoring Noelle as I pass her, ignoring the boys balls deep in club bunnies and the smell of weed and stale smoke in the air. This is home and usually it feels that way, but tonight, I'm a stranger in my own house.

Dog tired, I head up to the room I keep at the clubhouse. It's home and has been since Sasha left. I had the boys decorate it, so the walls are slate grey and the furniture is new. Other than the bed, there's a chest of drawers, wardrobe, a sofa and two bedside tables. Part of me wishes I'd kept the house I shared with Sash before she left. I may live and breathe my club, but sometimes, I need a break from dealing with all the shit and the shitheads that come with it. I should have kept it, but it was too hard seeing memories of her everywhere.

As I pass Sin's room, my eyes stray in that direction and my anger starts to grow. It takes everything in me to keep walking past, to not go in there and unleash hell again. I hate him for what he's done. Of all the people in my life, he's one of the few I trusted. He's also the only blood family I have left, so his betrayal cuts deep.

Once I've shut the door behind me, I slam my fist into the dry wall, cracking the plaster. I don't care about the decor, but I relish the trickle of blood that wends over my knuckles. the streaks of red are stark against the pale walls.

I shrug out of my kutte, draping it over the chair and then sag back onto the bed, still clothed.

As I lie there, my thoughts drift to a different time, to a time when it was me and Sasha versus the world.

Her being back is throwing me for a loop, one that is going to strangle us both.

7

SASHA

I WAKE in the chair at the side of the bed with a stiff neck and a hollow feeling in my gut. My eyes rise to take in the cot bed and the mass of blonde hair I can see. Lily-May is hanging on, fighting still, but I can see the toll this is taking on her little body. She needs this procedure and soon.

I push to my feet and move over to the bed, ignoring the beeping of the machines and the low light that is barely illuminating the room. I run my hand over her hair and she stirs a little.

"Mummy?"

"Baby, I'm here."

Lucy went to the canteen to get some breakfast for us both. She's been a godsend. I hate being alone in this room. It makes the reality of our situation more real.

Lily-May shifts and closes her eyes again. I'm grateful she can sleep through the worst, because knowing my daughter is suffering and is in pain that I can't fix is the worst kind of torture.

I kiss her head and leave the room once she drifts off again. I need coffee, although I'd prefer it with something a little stronger than milk. The vending machine in the corridor outside her room doesn't dispense the best cup of caffeine, but it's better than nothing.

I rub the back of my neck as I move towards the machine, my yawn tearing out of me. I could sleep for a month, but I don't have that option. I snatch an hour here and there, but I'm starting to feel the effects of running on near to empty.

As I push the button for a white coffee with sugar, I hear a voice behind me.

"Sasha."

Even after all this time, even after all the hurt, he has the power to make the apex between my legs throb with anticipation.

Slowly, I turn from the machine and come face to face with Rav. My heart twitches as I take him in. He looks the same as he did when I saw him at the compound, but he doesn't look like my Tyler, not anymore. He's bigger, brawnier and wears a permanent scowl etched onto his handsome face. His worn and battered kutte fits him like it's moulded to his frame, the 'President' patch on the front a stark reminder of the man he is.

Regret surges through me, followed by remorse. I shouldn't have let things get this far.

"Ty…" I breathe his name, trying to recapture my equilibrium. No one else can knock me off target like him. He still has the ability to bring me to my knees. He can still stir my desire and make me want him, even when he's snarling at me.

Today, his long dark hair is loose around his shoulders, which accentuates that beard he's wearing. He looks wild. It's a good look on him.

"Ravage," he growls. "I earned that name and you'll use it, like everyone else does."

And just like that ice fills my veins and my desire washes

away, because his words cut me to the bone. Once, I was the only person allowed to call him Tyler. Once, I knew everything there was to know about him. Now, he's treating me no better than a club bunny or an outsider, and fuck, does that hurt.

I steel myself, lifting my chin slightly, ignoring the pain his words bring.

"Ravage," I bite back, my stomach in knots at the malice in his tone. "They do the test down the hallway. I'll show you—"

I start to walk away, but he snags my bicep. An electric charge surges through me at his touch. My mind recalls our time spent together, the nights we spent making love and the days we spent talking about our future together—a future that is now destroyed.

"You said you'd explain." His voice is hard, unyielding.

Ice churns in my gut.

"And I will. Once you've done the test."

He shakes his head. "Explain first, then I'll do the test."

I swallow the bile that crawls up my throat. This is not a memory lane I want to take a walk back up. Rav says he wants the truth, but could he really handle knowing what his brother did to me?

He thinks this hurts now?

He has no idea the pain the truth will bring.

"There's not much to explain."

His gaze hardens. "He says you came on to him, that it was dark and he didn't know who you were."

I scoff at this. Sin's explanation sounds so crazy. "And you believe that?"

"No. I don't know what the fuck to believe. You left without a word, then you show back up years later telling me I might be a father, but so might my brother. What the fuck am I supposed to think?"

There's a hint of hurt beneath the angry words he fires at me. I should be sympathetic to that, but I'm not. I'm pissed off that he never once has taken my corner, that he hasn't fought for me. He keeps talking about our past, but he's seeing a different picture to the one I am. Yeah, I ran, but now I know it was the right decision.

Sin was right.

Rav wouldn't have believed me and I would not have been strong enough to fight them both back then.

I roll to my toes and get in his face, injustice and hurt making me furious. "You're supposed to know me better than anyone else," I hiss at him. "You know I would *never* cheat on you."

He gazes back at me, unflinchingly, his mouth pulling into a tight line. "The evidence suggests otherwise, darlin'."

I don't miss the sarcasm in his voice. It grates on my nerves. I didn't do shit wrong and I'm tired of paying for it. I'm tired of being the one called whore and slut, and whatever other words they use to bring me low—even if Sin made me feel like one.

"Then there's nothing to explain, is there?" I snap in his face.

Again, he doesn't react, other than a small draw down of his brows. I shake myself. This is not an argument I want to get into, even if Rav is bringing up all sorts of buried feelings. All I care about is my daughter.

"Are you going to do the test or not?" I demand, my patience wearing thin.

"I want to see her."

My heart rate kicks up a notch at his words. "No."

Maybe it's selfish to say it, considering the man could be her father, but I don't want any of the filth of my past to touch her, to taint her. It's unjust, since Rav never did a thing wrong, but he's still part of that other life—a life that built me up and then tore me down. It destroyed the girl I was, changed everything I thought about myself and left me with nightmares that still haunt me. It changed him too. There is plenty more darkness in him now.

His face contorts with rage.

"Sasha, if she's mine or there's even a hint she could be mine, I want to know my daughter, and if you think you're going to stop me—"

"You don't get a say in this. I raised her alone. I went through labour and night feeds and getting up when she was sick or scared. I'm the one who has sat with her in hospitals across London. Me. I did that. She's mine."

"You didn't exactly give me a fucking choice in that, babe." The 'babe' is said with venom behind it and it grinds on my already grated nerves.

"It was your fault I wa—" I cut myself off, not wanting to rehash the past. Not wanting to get into a debate with him.

"My fault, what?"

"Just forget it." When I start to turn away, he grabs my wrist. I drag my arm away, tired of being manhandled by him. He doesn't attempt to grab me again, but leans at the waist to get in my face.

"No, I won't just forget it. What the fuck happened between you two?"

I swallow down my disgust as memories flash across my mind. My skin still crawls, no matter how many hot showers I take. I can't erase Sin's touch. "Just do the test. Then I'll be out of your life again."

There's a begging tone to my voice that grates on my own nerves, and I can tell it grates on his too. I'm not someone who begs, ever, but for Lily-May, I will do whatever it takes.

"Whether you're in my life or not ain't your choice anymore, sweetheart."

"Rav—"

"No, you should have thought about that before your sweet mouth told me I could be a father." He pushes his fingers through his hair. "You take me to see her and I'll do your fucking test."

I'm backed into a corner here, and with no choice, I do the only thing I can. I agree.

"Okay. Follow me, but you do anything to upset her and I'll cut your fucking balls off."

8

RAVAGE

I'm on edge as I step into that room behind Sasha, my gaze lingering on the slim build of her hips and her narrow dainty shoulders that seem to carry the weight of the world on them. It's been years, but she still has the ability to make me hard just with a look, like some kind of fucking Siren. I hate that she can, but watching her brings back memories of our past, memories of a time when I thought I could do or be anything with her by my side.

Reality was far different.

Her hair, which was longer when we were together, is cut to her chin now. It suits her, but I miss the longer waves she had. It was the perfect length to wrap my fist in while fucking her from behind. This new look makes her seem harder, sharper even. Then again everything about her seems harder now, like life has chipped away at all her soft edges.

The urge to take her pouty mouth, to run my fingers through her hair, mark and claim her is overwhelming, but I keep it locked down. I keep my steel shutters up. I can't let her in, not even for a second.

I pull my gaze from her, and my stomach clenches as my

gaze roves around the room. I have no clue if this kid is mine or Sin's, but no child should end up somewhere like this. She should be running around doing kid things, not fighting for every next breath.

I want to be pissed about the fact this kid could be my brother's, but all my anger flees the moment I set my sight on her. Whatever happens, she's family, and that means something to me. Family is everything.

I move closer to the bed, peering down at her. The little girl is lying on her back, wires and tubes snaking out from under her pyjamas. She's tiny and delicate and everything me and Sasha are not—innocent.

There's a pallor to her already pale skin that tells me she's ill, and if it didn't, the machinery bleeping at the side of the cot bed, keeping her functioning, would.

The smell of antiseptics and cleaning fluids are heavy in the air, mingling with the scent of sickness. It's choking and I cough a little as I move towards the bed.

The kid doesn't wake as I stare into her face, trying to see me in her features, but while there are some noticeable attributes that I could say come from my side of the family, she's Sash in miniature—apart from the hair colouring.

My eyes move to the board over the bed where 'Lily-May Montgomery' is scrawled. That pisses me off. She should be a Jenkins. There shouldn't be any doubt about who her father is.

I jump down on my anger. Now is not the time to let rip. Even so, what-if scenarios race through my mind as I think about the life I could have had if Sash hadn't been unfaithful, if my brother hadn't betrayed me. It would be me sitting at this kid's bedside, doing everything I could to keep her breathing.

I understand Sasha's determination to get us tested. If she is mine, I'd walk on fire for her.

If she is mine, I will.

Looking at her, it's impossible to tell either way. I look too much like Sin to see past the familial similarities.

Sasha doesn't offer any words or explanations. She just stands on the other side of the bed, running her fingers over her daughter's hair.

"The transplant will help?" I ask.

"It's her last chance. I already tested, but I'm not a full match. Her father might be, though."

My jaw clenches at this information as I think of her with Sin. I should have murdered that little fucker.

The urge to spit vitriol at her is squashed by the little girl sleeping in the bed. She tempers my response.

Unable to stand there any longer, conjuring pictures of what our future could have looked like, conjuring images of the thing that tore us apart, I stride from the room, raking my fingers through my hair.

As soon as I'm in the hallway, my hands go to the back of my neck and I stare up at the ceiling as I roar out a, "Fuck!"

Sasha doesn't say a word. She watches my outburst with a quiet disinterest that pisses me off. I'd rather she spit venom back. That would give me a reason to offload all this anger inside me.

"I want a paternity test." Saying these words loosens some of the heaviness in my chest, but the ripple of panic that goes across her face confuses me.

Shouldn't she want to know this too?

"No."

"I wasn't asking, darlin'. I want that test."

I watch her throat work as she shakes her head, her guard coming down for long enough to let me see the vulnerability beneath. She's scared. Not just scared, but petrified.

Why the fuck would she be petrified of finding out who the father is?

I don't like puzzles, especially ones I can't solve, and this only adds to my suspicion that something more is going on.

"It's in the past, Rav. What difference does it make?"

"She's two and a half years old. I have the rest of my life to be her dad if she's mine, so yeah, Sash, it makes all the fucking difference."

I watch her teeth grit before she loosens her jaw.

"Fine," she concedes. "You do the bone marrow test and I'll have a paternity test done. Deal?"

I nod. Then point a finger at her chest. "There's more going on here than you're letting on and you're going to give me the answers, even if I have to drag them out of you."

She lets out a frustrated breath. "There's nothing going on here. Stop trying to find reasons and just accept it happened. I have."

I stare at her, trying to get the lay of the situation and then my lip curls into a snarl. "Now's the time to come clean if something else went on."

She meets my angry gaze with a defiant one and mutters out a, "Do the test. They managed to squeeze you in this morning. I can't guarantee another slot."

Her hedging is pissing me off, but she's a closed door to me. I shake my head.

"I'll do it because that little girl in there is family, but we're not done here. Not by a long shot."

I stride up the corridor towards the nurses' station and lean my elbows on the top of the reception desk. The nurse's eyes raise to mine and I see a flash of fear as she takes in my size and my kutte. It's a reaction I'm used to. Women swing between scared and interested by my kutte. This one is the former.

She swallows hard and asks, "Yes?"

"I'm here to do the test for Lily-May Montgomery."

"Oh, right. Absolutely."

She fumbles about with a stack of paperwork then leads me into a side room.

"It's a simple procedure. We just swab the inside of your cheek." She's trying to reassure me, but I'm not in the mood for chit chat or small talk.

"Let's just get this over with, yeah?"

She nods and orders me to sit at the side of the desk. I take my seat and wait while she gloves up and gets the equipment she needs out.

"Okay, open wide."

I open my mouth and she scrapes the swab across the inside of my cheek.

"All done."

I watch as she places the swab in a vial and smiles at me.

"It'll take a couple of days for the results to come back."

"Yeah, thanks," I mutter, getting to my feet.

I push out the room and go in search of Sasha, determined more than ever to get my answers.

9

RAVAGE

Lily-May's room is shut up tight, a bunch of doctors on the other side when I come back from doing the test. I can see Sasha's back through the small pane of glass in the door. I'm contemplating entering the room when a voice behind me says, "They'll be done in a minute."

I turn, coming face to face with a small blonde woman who is glaring at me like I kill puppies in my spare time. She's clutching a paper bag, two bottles of water on the chair next to her.

I let my gaze rove over her lazily, enjoying the way she squirms under my scrutiny, even though she tries not to. She's got balls, I'll give her that. Most people would be freaked the fuck out by me, but not her—at least not outwardly. She's hiding her fear well.

"You're Ravage, right?" she questions, her head tilted to one side as she takes me in. Her mouth pulls into a slight sneer as she straightens her back, but I don't miss the fear dancing behind her eyes and the tremble in her hands.

I don't answer her, instead firing back my own question.

"And you are?"

"Lucy. Sash and Lily-May live with me."

So, this is the bitch Sasha has been hiding with? I can see why. She's strong and has an edge to her. I'm not sure why I'm supposed to give a fuck, or why she's introduced herself, but the woman isn't finished yet.

"She just got herself back together. Back off and stop giving her shit."

"And what the fuck has it got to do with you?" I pull my lips into a sneer, baring my teeth. "Who's going to stop me? You?" I snort.

"Sasha is my friend, and I was the one who had to pick up the broken pieces. Leaving you nearly fucking killed her."

The accusation in her voice has my anger flaring. "She was broken? I was the one she walked out on without a word." I grit my teeth. "I'm only here because that kid in there might be mine. I don't give a fuck about Sasha."

That's a lie, but it's one I'm going to keep telling myself. I fucking hate her, but I also care about her, and that's the fucking problem. Things would be easier if I didn't.

Lucy glares up at me, her eyes shooting venom. "You and that fucking club destroyed her, and we both know Sasha isn't the type of woman to break easily. You should have seen her. She wouldn't eat, she cried all the time. I was the one who glued her back together while she was dealing with her pregnancy. You think you're hard done by? You should have lived through what she had to. So yeah, I have every fucking right."

"She fucked my brother," I hiss at her. If we weren't in a public place, I might have let my temper go fully. As it is, I'm struggling to keep a tight rein on it.

She laughs at my words although I see a hint of fear dancing in her eyes as her gaze shifts around the hallway.

"Is that what that bastard said?" she demands, then shakes

her head. Disgust crosses her face. "And you believed him, didn't you?"

"There's a kid in there that could be either mine or my brother's. Do you need a lesson in fucking biology?"

"I hope he rots in hell. Fuck, I'd send him there myself."

"What the fuck? Are you threatening my brother?

"Your brother is a piece of shit, Ravage. And trust me, if I ever see him it won't be a threat."

Sin is a bastard, but that doesn't mean I'll let some bit of skirt threaten him. I step into her space and I watch the fear flicker in her eyes as she tries not to shrink back in her seat.

"Watch your fucking mouth."

We're so busy smarting off at each other that neither of us notice the door opening and the doctors filing out until Sasha demands, "What the hell is going on?"

I give her friend a dark glare before I turn to Sasha.

"I was just getting to know your housemate."

Sasha's eyes slide towards Lucy and again, I glimpse her discomfort and uncertainty for a moment before the walls come back up. She was never this closed off to me before. I hate that she is now because it makes it hard as hell to read her.

I jut my chin towards the room. "What's going on?"

"Just the doctor's rounds. You did the test?"

"Yeah, Sash. I did the test. Time to explain things."

"I already explained. I'm not going over this again. It's done. We're no longer the same people anymore, so just leave it."

I clench my jaw. "Then there's nothing else to fucking say, is there?"

I head out to the car park and climb on my bike. It's a beautiful machine, all chrome and custom painted along the fuel tank. The power of the machine between my legs as I start it up reminds me who I am and what I'm about. As I rev the engine, I feel my anger melt away a little. A ride will clear my head, so instead of turning right out of the hospital entrance and heading back towards the clubhouse, I take a left and head for the ring road. The traffic is busy but moving, and I lane split to keep my wheels spinning. The urge to hit the open road and not look back is overwhelming, but the Untamed Sons are not without enemies. Leaving the territory without a properly planned route is dangerous, and I have no intention of calling my road captain, Titch, and asking for those details. Instead, I just ride aimlessly around Kessington until I feel the rage leaving me enough to return to the clubhouse.

Zack, the kid on the gate, lets me through and I pull my bike into my space near the front doors. As I kick down the stand, my head is full of the shit that happened at the hospital. I'm more convinced than ever that something more went on between Sin and Sasha, but getting anything out of her is impossible.

I stride across the tarmac and into the clubhouse to find the common room almost empty. Fury is sitting in the corner, staring at nothing.

"Where the hell is everyone?" I ask him.

His eyes raise to meet mine and I see the moment his demons back down in them and he comes into the present.

"A run."

"Why aren't you with them?"

"They don't trust me to be… calm."

He doesn't say this with any malice, but just states it as a fact.

I trust my brothers, though, so if Fury didn't get an invite to the party, there's a good reason for it. I arch a brow, blow out a breath and then head for the bar. Melody slips behind it, flicking her red hair. She doesn't ask what I want to drink, just reaches for the top shelf Scotch and pours me a good measure before sliding it in front of me.

"Thanks, sweetheart."

She beams at the praise, ducking her head, so her hair curtains her face. These bitches are like little girls, seeking daddy's approval. It's pathetic.

I knock the drink back in one go and slide the glass back on the bar. When Melody moves to pour me another, I shake my head. She's nothing like Sasha was at her age. She was bold, ballsy and didn't take shit. These club bunnies just roll over every time someone speaks to them.

"I'm done."

I push up from the bar and head to my office and once I'm in the quiet of the room, I let my mind go back to that day—the day Sasha left me. I ignore the quagmire of pain I'm wading through and try to recall exactly what the fuck happened in the run up to her walking out.

And the only thing I can remember is I sent my brother on a protection detail—to take care of Sash while I was out of town for the afternoon.

Fuck. Did I push them together?

SASHA

LILY-MAY WAKES for a few hours and is fussy. I'm shredded watching my child suffer. Every whimper breaks my heart. Every tear tears me apart. The pain I see in her eyes is like a knife to the gut. If I could trade places with her, I would in a heartbeat.

Sitting at her bedside, watching her toss and turn, gives me too much time to think about the past and what happened. I told Rav I would get a paternity test done if he did the test for Lily-May, but I haven't done anything yet. It doesn't feel good to have gone back on my word, but I'm fucking terrified of finding out the truth. My skin hasn't stopped crawling since Rav brought it up. She can't be Sin's. He doesn't get to dirty any part of *my* daughter. If Rav isn't her dad it would break me even more. Sin took so fucking much. I won't let him take this too. The truth will give Rav or Sin power in her life, and I will kill Sin before I allow him anywhere near her.

I close my eyes, trying to calm my cantering heart, and push out the dark thoughts creeping into my mind. If she's

Sin's, it won't change anything about how I love my daughter, but for her sake I hope her father isn't a monster.

There's a knock on the door and both me and Lucy glance towards it. Through the glass, I can see the outline of someone I never expected to see here.

Nox.

He doesn't wait for us to grant him access, but pushes inside as if he owns the place.

Lucy comes to her feet, stepping between us, a circus ringmaster standing between the lion and the audience. Her intention is sweet, but unnecessary. I'm not scared of Nox.

His eyes crawl over my face as he takes me in. I feel like he's trying to pull all my secrets from the deepest of my vaults with that look. I keep my shutters pulled firmly down.

"No, no more Untamed Sons," Lucy says, although I hear the tremble in her words.

Nox's eyes move over her body with a lingering look that has his mouth quirking at the corners, pulling into a smirk.

"And who are you?"

Before things get out of hand, I intervene, stepping forward.

"What are you doing here?" I demand.

His expression turns serious. "I want to talk."

I arch my brow at him. "Now you want to talk? You weren't that open to the idea the last time I saw you."

"Shit changes."

He stares at me, his gaze hard and unyielding until I glance away. I don't like the way he's looking at me, as if he's seeing past the bullshit to the scared, broken girl underneath.

"I'm kind of busy, Nox."

My hand goes to my daughter's stomach and he watches the movement with an unreadable expression.

"It won't take a second."

I don't want to leave Lily-May, but he's not going to get

out of my hair until I talk to him, so I let out a huff and mutter to Lucy, "Stay with Lil."

Tingles fill my stomach as I follow him out of the room, my eyes locked on the Untamed Sons insignia filling the back of his kutte—a crowned skull wearing a pair of wings, the top rocker reading 'Untamed Sons', the bottom 'London'. What the hell does he want to talk about?

He leads me out into the corridor and then out of the main entrance to the outside seating area. There's no one about, so he signals for me to take a seat on the bench furthest from the entrance. I do, but only because I want this shit over fast, so I can get back to my daughter.

"I've been thinking a lot about things since I saw you last."

"Did you come all this way to tell me that?" I snap at him.

"Sash, I know you. I've known you pretty much my whole fucking life. We grew up in this club together."

Cold swamps me at his words.

"So what? Shit changes." I throw his earlier words back at him, which earns me a frustrated glare.

"I know you're hiding something about what the fuck happened between you and Sin."

Glacial fingers crawl over my skin at his words. I don't want him digging around in the past. I want to forget what happened. I don't want to relive that nightmare.

"I've got nothing to hide. It happened. I left. End of story."

He doesn't let it go, as I expect. If anything, he becomes more persistent. "I know you, Sash. And I know him. He's lying out of his arse, but you're lying too. I want to know why."

"I thought he told you what happened," I sneer at him, squirming internally at where this conversation is heading.

"Yeah, well, I'm asking you." He huffs out a breath as his eyes lock on mine. "If something happened, we need to know."

Cold swamps me at his words and I lean forwards on the bench, clasping my hands in my lap in an attempt to hide they're trembling. I don't want to go down this path, not with my child struggling in a hospital bed. All I want to focus on is Lily-May. I can't deal with this, too. I can't deal with being so close to the club, with seeing Rav and the brothers. Seeing Sin. I thought I could, but I was wrong.

My walls are fracturing at the look in his eyes. The stress of dealing with Lily being so sick, of dealing with Rav and facing Sin, of having someone probing at my defences is making me weaker. It's too fucking much. I'm strong, but even the strongest person can break under the right pressure. Hard words I can take. Rav's hatred, I can handle, because I hate me too. Sin lying I can deal with because it lets me hide under the blanket of denial, but Nox looking at me with softness swirling behind the stone cold glare is what finally breaks me.

A lone tear streaks down my cheek.

"Just leave it alone, Nox, okay?"

"No, not okay. Where did it happen? How did it happen?"

"I don't remember."

I do remember. I remember every fucking detail of that night. It's branded into my soul.

"You don't remember fucking your old man's brother?"

I don't answer as a flashback from that night dances in front of me. The sounds he made as he pumped into me, the way he held my wrists down as he took what wasn't his to take. I'm going to splinter into a thousand pieces if Nox keeps this up.

"How did you end up shagging? Tell me," he interrupts my thoughts and my defences shatter like a mirror.

My breath hitches. "It wasn't—"

"Did you seduce him first? Was it dark, like he said?"

"Yes," I gasp. The room had been pitch-black. There were

no lights on, which made everything else heightened. I remember the sound of his breath, his belt dropping, the taste of my salty tears.

I'm struggling to breathe as more memories flood me.

"Did he make the first move?"

"Stop! Please... stop!" I fist my hands over my ears, trying to block his words out.

"You didn't fuck him, did you?" He pauses and it feels like the world takes a breath before he says, "He raped you."

My whole body jolts at his words. Pain lances through my chest as my skin crawls. The dirt I've tried so hard to wash away for years is suddenly covering me and I can't hide it any longer.

Another tear falls, then another.

"Nox, please. I'm begging you."

"Sash, he raped you, didn't he?" he presses, ignoring my pleas. "That's why you can't stand the sight of him. That's why you ran. I fucking knew something was going on. You were the most loyal woman. There's no way in hell you'd willingly fuck Sin, and you'd never leave Rav unless you didn't have a choice."

I surge to my feet and he follows me up, all six-foot-three of him towering over my smaller frame. Without thought, I shove at his chest hard, but he doesn't move an inch. Then I scream in his face, "I told you to leave it alone!"

He takes this without a word, before his face contorts into a mask of rage that has my stomach twisting. I see the anger burning in his eyes as he takes me in and for the first time, I feel fear.

"I'm going to gut him."

My brows draw together as realisation dawns, as Sin's lies fall apart. He told me no one would listen. He told me no one would care. He told me no one would ever believe a filthy

65

slut like me, but Nox is here, spitting fire and standing in my corner.

Disbelief makes my words come out breathy as I peer up at him through watery eyes. "You believe me?"

"Yeah, I believe you." He tears a hand over the scruff of hair covering his head and roars a, "Fuck!" into the air.

My arms wrap around my middle as I watch him unravel, my breath dragging out of me in heavy pants as more tears threaten to fall. He steps towards me and wraps his thick arms around me, squeezing me until my ribs hurt.

"That fucking cunt is dead," he whispers against my hair. It's not a threat. I know Nox can fulfil that promise and fear swamps me.

I shake my head. "You can't tell anyone else. Promise me."

He pulls back and glares at me with disbelief. "No fucking way am I promising that."

I grab at his arm and shake him. "Please."

His jaw tightens and his eyes blaze. I step back a little. "He has to pay. He never had the right to do that. Not to you. Fuck, Sash, never to you. He signed his own death when he put his hands on something that didn't belong to him."

He grabs my face, using his thumb to wipe away a few stray tears.

"You might have belonged to Rav, but you belonged to the club too. We all loved you. You were family. And no fucker messes with family, even that bastard."

I shake my head, trying to clear the blood pounding in my ears. "Just because you believe me doesn't mean anyone else will. Rav's never going to believe his little brother…" I break off, unable to say the words that make me feel unclean. I lick my lips. "No one will believe me over Sin."

His brows knit together. "Is that what he told you? Is that the shit he made you believe?" Nox paces in front of me, his steps sharp. The anger rolling off him is barely contained.

Desperation dogs my steps now. This can't come out. No one can know my dirty secret.

"He was right. Look at what's happened since I've been back. No one doubted him! It was me they all called a fucking slut, a fucking whore! It's me Rav hates! They all believe him!"

"I believe you, and no one believed Sin's bullshit story." He clenches his jaw and mutters another, "Fuck!" before his eyes come back to me. "He's why you left. He's why you don't know who the father of your kid is."

I feel laid bare to him, naked, and I don't like it. I want to build my walls back up and protect myself, but the bricks are gone and there's no way to fix this. Now that this secret is out there, there's no hiding it. Shame crawls over me. I close my eyes, the only thing I can do to block this out.

"Rav needs to know."

My eyes pop open as panic attacks me.

"No."

"Yeah, Sash. He deserves to know why you walked out."

"No matter the reason, I still left him. I still turned my back on him. Do you think this will change that fact? He hates me. Why make it worse?"

"This changes everything."

"You can't tell him."

"Yeah, sweetheart, I can. I'm not keeping something this big from my president—from my friend."

My chin wobbles as more tears threaten. I need to get hold of myself, but I can't. I'm unravelling as fast as Nox is. I never thought anyone would find out the truth and I feel soiled by it.

"Nox, please. He'll never get over his brother betraying him. Sin's his only family. Me, he already hates, and I'll take that hate, if it saves Rav from knowing the truth."

"I meant what I said. Sin's going to pay for this," Nox tells me. "This won't go unpunished."

He strides off towards the car park, kicking a trash can as he goes. It doesn't move, probably screwed into the ground, but I hear his roared curse and shiver.

I let him go. I don't think I could stop him anyway. He's on the warpath.

Tears clog my throat as I watch him walk away. Just because he believed me, doesn't mean Ravage will.

But now everyone will know my secret.

Because Nox isn't going to keep this quiet. Nox isn't going to let Sin off the hook.

Which means everyone is going to find out how I was overpowered and defiled by a man I was supposed to be able to trust.

Fuck.

RAVAGE

THE COMMON ROOM is full of brothers, club bunnies and a few regular hangarounds. There's a buzz in the air, a party atmosphere as the booze flows freely and the girls make the rounds. Noelle is straddling Levi—the club's secretary—his jeans halfway around his thighs, as she bounces up and down on his cock, her head thrown back as she moans. Her skirt is rucked up around her hips showing the globes of her arse and one tit is exposed as Levi plays with it.

On the other sofa, Melody is giving head to Titch. Her cheeks hollow out every time she moves up and down his shaft and his eyes are squeezed shut in the throes of ecstasy.

Across the room, Daimon is standing by the pool table with Whizz and a couple of other brothers, while Fury watches on from the sidelines, his brows drawn together. I don't want to think what is going through that fucker's head right now.

The only person missing is my brother, that backstabbing bastard—Sin.

It's a good thing. How I feel right now, I might slit his fucking throat.

I try to drown out Noelle's mewls as she reaches her climax and gesture to Kyle behind the bar to turn the music up. I don't need to hear her screaming, and Noelle is vocal.

The smell of pussy, weed and cigarettes is heavy in the air. It soothes the demons in me, pushes them back down to safer levels. This is home, and this is just another normal Wednesday night for the club.

This is also what I love about my club. No one tells us what to do or how to do it. No one judges our decisions, unless they affect the club directly. If you want to fuck a bunny in the middle of the room, that's your fucking choice. No one will say shit about it.

I focus on my Scotch, wondering if I should take advantage of all the free pussy in the room and fuck the anger away, getting lost for just a few moments between some bunny's legs. I'm still seething after seeing Sasha. That bitch is lying to me and it's pissing me off that I can't figure out why.

I take a sip of my drink and try to get control of myself. I hate that she can affect me this way, that I can be this out of my mind because of her. I wish she'd never come back. Every time I see her, I struggle between wanting to fuck her and wanting to kill her.

The doors of the common room bang open, drawing my attention. I twist on the stool and see Nox standing there, his fists clenched at his side. His wild eyes roam the room, looking like he's about to commit an atrocity, before they land on me. I don't like what I see in his glare. I don't like the malice he's directing at me.

My senses go on alert, and I signal to Kyle to turn the music off as I slide off my stool. I've known Nox my entire life. I know how he ticks. I know when he's pissed off, too, and right now he's spitting fire, the flames of hell burning through him.

His mouth curls into a snarl that has me guarded. I'm not sure where this fucker's head is at. We don't match in size, but if we got into it, blood would be drawn, bones would be broken.

"Where is he?" Nox snarls out, each word punching through the tension gathering heavily in the air.

The entire room stops and focuses their attention on the man spewing venom from the doorway. I don't take my gaze off him, but I can feel my brothers shifting closer, ready to take him down if things get out of hand.

"Where's who?" I spit out. I'm not happy about the way he's talking to me, but I can sense something more is going on here, something I want to understand. I've seen Nox angry over the years, but this is something else.

"Sin," he roars. The danger radiating from him is lethal.

Instinct flares to life inside me, warning me to tread carefully here. Whatever is going on, Nox is not level. If his words weren't an indication, the way he's flexing his fists and the snarl on his face are.

"Why?"

"I'm going to fucking kill him."

Old protective urges to keep my little brother safe come to the surface briefly, before they're doused. I don't owe that little bastard anything—least of all my protection. I do want to know why one of my best men wants him dead, though.

"Explain," I demand.

Nox doesn't. He turns on his heel and strides from the room, but not before he clears a table of glasses with a sweeping of his hand.

What the fuck?

I scrub a hand down my face as Fury comes up off the wall where he's leaning. I shake my head. I can handle Nox alone and I have the feeling this is not a conversation I want to have with an audience.

My stomach clenches as I jog after him, following the trail of destruction he's leaving as he stalks through the clubhouse. The brother is moving quickly, with purpose and I can see the demons tailing him as he goes. Whatever has happened it's big.

He reaches Sin's door and doesn't bother to knock. He puts a boot to the door and kicks it in.

The sound of wood splintering is loud in the quiet of the corridor. I glance at the broken shards of wood, my brain struggling to comprehend why he's so pissed. What the fuck happened between now and earlier?

I step through the mess of the door that looks like shredded firewood, keeping one eye locked on his back.

Nox's face contorts into a mask of rage as he takes in the crumpled mess of blankets on the bed and the medical supplies littering the bedside table. There are bloodied rags in the trash can, but the air smells stale—like no one has been in here for a few days.

My gaze stops on the drawers of the dresser. They're pulled open and are empty, as if they were cleared in a hurry.

Nox strides to the wardrobe and yanks the doors open. Then yells a, "Fuck!"

There's no clothes in there either.

Little bastard. He's running.

I feel my own rage move to dangerous levels. How the fuck did he get out of the compound?

Someone is going to pay for that.

Nox rounds on me, fisting his fingers into my kutte and slamming me against the wall.

"Where the fuck is he?" Nox demands, his eyes burning fire.

"Take your fucking hands off me before I kill you," I snarl at him.

He releases me with a shove and steps back, his hands going to the back of his head.

"You find him, Rav, and you find him fast."

My temper flares at his words, and I push down the monster threatening to surface long enough to snap out a, "Remember who the fuck you're talking to!"

If this bothers him, he doesn't show it and that scares me. Nox is loyal. I'd trust him with my life and the life of every man in this clubhouse. Him putting his hands on me, losing control like this, isn't him.

What the fuck is going on?

Nox runs a hand over his face and I can see him unravelling in front of my eyes. He's barely keeping his shit together. He points a finger in my direction and growls under his breath, "I'm going to kill him."

"Threatening another brother without reason could lose you your colours." I let the warning hang between us. Sin might be on my shit list right now, but the bylaws are still the bylaws. You don't put hands on another brother with intent to maim or kill without a fucking good reason—like fucking your old lady.

He stands there, hands on hips, staring at the ceiling as if his entire life has just imploded in front of his eyes. Then he dips his head and meets my gaze before grinding out, "That sick bastard raped Sasha."

The words hang heavily in the silence. I hear them, but I don't compute them for a moment. When I do, nausea swirls in my gut and pain starts to build behind my eyes. I thought seeing red was just a phrase, but my vision is clouded with crimson.

"That's why she fucking left! Not because she fucking cheated. He *raped* her."

The rage, the fury, the demons I can't ever exorcise, rise in me at his words.

"What?" I growl out the word, tasting ash on my tongue, the bitterness of a betrayal so vile I can't even comprehend my brother would do this.

"He fucking raped her," he repeats.

"You're lying." I can't believe him. Believing him would mean my brother's death—a brother I raised, a brother I loved. If it's true, there's no way in fuck I'm letting him stay breathing. If it's true, I'll put a bullet in his head myself.

Thoughts of Sasha before she left dance across my mind —the carefree woman I loved. I see none of that in this new version of her. She's hard, jaded, pissed at the world.

And now I know why.

If it's true…

I don't want to believe it, but I can see the truth in Nox's stance. He believes it.

"You don't think I wish it wasn't true? He's a brother," he says, his voice ravaged, "but I heard it from Sasha's mouth. It's not a lie."

My arms fold over my broad chest as I take this in, still not willing to believe it, not willing to deal with the fallout of what that would mean, desperately needing it to be wrong.

"She's a deceitful bitch. Why the fuck are you believing a word that comes out of her lying whore mouth over a brother?"

Nox's fist lashes out, landing on my jaw. I see stars for a second as I go back on a foot, my jaw burning from the pressure of the hit.

"You're a fucking bastard."

Anger swirls in my gut.

"She fucked my brother. What else am I supposed to call her?"

Nox glares at me like I'm shit under his shoe. "Do you really not remember anything? Has your pride fucking blinded you that much? Sasha would never have betrayed you. We all know it. You know it. She was loyal as fuck to you. You were everything to her. Anyone with a pair of eyes could tell how much she loved you."

Sasha was loyal. Until she wasn't. But a tendril of doubt is starting to make its way through me. The way she acted towards Sin, the way she's acted since she came back. She never once has admitted fucking him either. She always hedged around it.

"If it's true, why the fuck didn't she say?"

"Because this was her fear! That you wouldn't believe her. I watched that woman break down and shatter telling me what happened. She ain't lying, Rav. He fucking hurt her." His arms gesture to the empty room. "And if he didn't do shit, where is he? Why run? He took his beating. It was done. My thoughts are he couldn't chance you and Sasha talking. He couldn't risk anyone figuring out what he did. He ran because he's a fucking lying, betraying piece of shit rapist."

I don't trust myself to speak yet. Did Sin do it? Did he rape the woman I loved? Is that why she left?

The pieces of the puzzle start to fall into place and I really don't like where the hell they're falling.

My temper fractures and I let my frustration free. I tug over the drawers and then I go to work on beating the shit out of everything I can touch.

When I'm done, I'm breathing heavily, my breath ripping out of me, blood running over my knuckles again. I point at Nox.

"You're sure about this?"

"Yeah."

I turn my head away, running my fingers through my hair as I step over the mess to fall into the chair at the side of the bed. This life is dark. It comes with unspeakable crimes and it's filled with blood. I can handle anything this world throws at me, but not this. Fuck, never this.

He raped my girl. He fucking hurt her and broke her beautiful spirit. All I can see is her scared, destroyed. Was she screaming for me? Calling my name?

He violated her in the worst way.

A lone tear rolls down my face as I look towards Nox.

"What have I done?"

Nox's voice softens as he says, "Rav... you couldn't have known."

I shake my head, climbing over the mess towards the door.

"Where are you going?"

"To see Sasha."

A storm is starting to brew inside me, building off my fury. An eerie calm comes over me.

"Then I'm going hunting."

We both know who I'm talking about.

Run, Sin, because I'm coming for you.

SASHA

I HOLD my daughter in my arms for the first time in days. She's rubbing at her eyes, her exhaustion marring every line in her face. I can't bear seeing her broken down like this, and it takes everything I have to keep my emotions in check. I have to be strong for her, even though I'm running on empty myself.

Lucy went home an hour ago to shower before she has to head to work. Her company deals with acquisitions of other companies, and although she's pretty low on the food chain there she loves it. I have no clue how she's still functioning, but somehow she is. I feel wrecked. I couldn't do a full day's work on top of this. She's super human.

I place Lily-May back in the cot bed and straighten her pyjamas before running a hand over her head. She feels warm, clammy. Waiting for Rav's test to come back is a special kind of torture. I hope like hell he can help my daughter. The thought he might not be a match sits like a weight in the pit of my stomach, a weight I try to ignore.

The door pushes open behind me and I twist to look. My stomach both flips and clenches as I see Ravage standing in the doorway. Instantly, my guard goes up. The look in his eyes shreds me. There's pain there, raw pain that hits me in the gut and makes me forget I'm pissed at him.

Last time I saw him he was spitting fire at me, now he looks broken as he stands there, staring at me, as if he's seeing into the depths of my soul.

I swallow past the lump in my throat, icy claws wrapping around my heart as he takes a step into the room. I can barely breathe as his eyes crawl over my face, looking for what, I don't know. He must not find it, though, because he pulls his eyes from me and flicks his gaze towards the bed.

I shift slightly, putting my body between my daughter and Rav. I don't think he'd hurt her, but I can't get a read on his state of mind right now, and that terrifies me more than if he'd come in here spewing venom. At least then I'd know where I stand.

"What are you doing here?" I ask, my words coming out in a breathy whisper.

Every synapse in my body is snapped to attention, firing electric charges throughout my body.

He doesn't speak, but moves to the bed. I shift, ready for whatever is about to happen next, but he doesn't do anything except peer down at her. Lily-May watches him from beneath heavy lids, her long lashes fanning over her cheeks as her eyes shutter closed and sleep claims her. Seeing her with him has my walls start to pull down. Everything in me hopes he's her daddy, that the filth of my past hasn't marred my daughter too. It's an ache that gnaws at my gut until nausea rises in my throat.

"Rav?" His silence has me on edge and I tighten my grip on the rail of the cot. Why the fuck isn't he speaking?

"Did the results come back yet?" he finally asks, his voice sounding raw. My brows draw together as I try to get a read on him, and fail.

"Tomorrow."

I watch him cautiously, unsure what his next move will be, but when his eyes come back to mine, I see the remorse, the guilt and cold washes over me.

He knows the truth.

Nox told him what Sin did to me.

My throat constricts as if someone has a hand wrapped around my neck and I struggle to draw breath. He can't know. No one can.

Filth crawls over my skin as I stand in front of him, laid bare as he sees beneath my carefully crafted walls. They shatter at the same time I do. Tears brim in my eyes before I let them fall.

"You know." There's a hint of accusation in my tone, a hint of anger too, although I'm not sure if that's directed at him or me.

Panic swamps my belly when he doesn't answer. Does he believe me?

"Nox told you—"

I barely get my words out before I'm dragged into his arms and engulfed by his hard body. I stiffen for a second before I melt against him, smelling his aftershave, the leather of his kutte. All my fear, all my hurt is soothed by the feel of his thick grasp around my body. God, how I've missed this. I burrow into his chest, letting my tears fall freely now and he squeezes me tightly against him.

For the first time in years, I feel safe surrounded by him. He chips away at the dirt covering me, just long enough for me to take a lifesaving breath.

My hands snake around his back, clinging to him like I'm scared to let him go. I am. I don't want to see pity in his eyes. I don't want him to look at me differently.

His fingers thread into the hair at the nape of my neck, as

his nose brushes through the strands on top and he breathes into it.

"I can't fix what he's done, but he'll pay for it. I promise you that," he assures me on a quiet, but deadly breath.

I tighten my hold on him and press my cheek to his chest. Being back in his arms after all this time feels right, good. I've missed him holding me. I've missed him touching me. I don't want this to ever end, but he pulls me back from him and the moment shatters. The warmth from his body disappears, leaving me cold to the bone.

He peers down at me, and with gentleness I'm not sure I deserve, he uses the pad of his thumb to wipe my tears from my cheeks.

"You should have told me." There's chastisement in his tone.

"He's your family. Would you have believed me?" My voice is pitched low, soft, filled with remorse.

He dips his head and presses his lips to my forehead. It's a gesture that's intimate and has my eyes closing as I embrace his unspoken words. Rav has never been good at talking about his feelings. He's a biker. They don't do emotions, but his actions tell me the depth of feeling he has right now. It tells me how ravaged he is by what he's learnt, and more importantly, it tells me he believes me—something Sin said would never happen. I believed that with every painful breath as I walked away, but I should have believed in the man in front of me. Rav has always protected me. Why did Sin's words have the power to make me doubt him?

That's when it hits me. Sin made me feel powerless. He took away my safe place and made me doubt the world around me, the men that cared for me. For the first time in my life, he showed me what fear really was, but he was wrong. So fucking wrong.

I spent the past three years, doing it alone, when I could

have had Rav at my side. We could have raised Lily-May together.

The thought breaks something inside of me as I remember every time I wished he was there: the fear and pain I felt bringing her into this world, when she took her first steps, when the doctor first told me she was sick…

One question bobs to the surface of my thoughts. Could he ever accept her as his own?

I push that thought into the darkest, deepest of my vaults and shut the door on it. Lily-May can't help how she was conceived, and I'll never make my child feel anything but loved. If Rav can't get on board with that then he has no place in our life.

"Knowing he touched—" He breaks off, gritting his teeth so hard, it makes my own hurt. "It fucking guts me, Sasha."

His words blanket me in relief as much as they cause me pain. I hate that he's hurting too. This has to be destroying him, but the fact he believes me unlocks the heaviness in my chest that I've carried around for years.

"Rav…" There's so much weight in that small word, so much I want to say but can't. "I should have told you. I shouldn't have believed Sin. It killed me walking away."

"I know," is all he says, as if he can see all my thoughts.

"What happens now?" I ask, pulling back slightly so I can peer up at his face.

His mouth pulls into a sneer.

"Now, I find Sin."

"Find him?" My heart twitches at his words. I take another step back.

I watch Rav's jaw work. "He took off."

Panic floods my belly and my breath starts to quicken, but Rav cups my face with his ringed hands. "He's not going to touch you again—or Lily-May. I promise, I'll protect you both."

I want to believe that, I really do, but I thought I was safe in the past and that wasn't the case. I don't say this to Rav. He's barely hanging on as it is, but the thoughts dance across my consciousness.

I'll never be safe while Sin is out there.

And neither will my daughter.

RAVAGE

Seeing Sasha break is like a blade to the gut, twisted deep inside me. I didn't expect her tears. Each one is like a bullet to the heart. She's always been so strong, but the woman in front of me now is nothing like the woman who left me. She's harder in many ways. Her eyes are filled with distrust, hurt mixing with her fear, but there's a vulnerability there that I never noticed before.

I didn't want to believe my brother could be capable of the things he did to her. I didn't think he could be so sick and fucking twisted. Sash can hide a lot of things behind the walls she's put up, but the tears that fell down her cheeks don't lie. The way her fucking body trembled in my arms couldn't be faked or forced. As much as I don't want to believe that the boy I raised is a fucking rapist, I know he did it. Everything in my gut is telling me he's guilty, that he laid his hands on her. I can see the truth in her eyes. I don't know how I missed it before. I recognise the newly formed demons in hers, because they match the ones in mine. I never wanted my girl to have any monsters in her life, and I led this monster to her front door. I'll never forgive myself.

Uncertainty clings to her as she peers up at me, searching for direction on where we go next. I'm not sure of that either. How can she look at me and not see his fucking face?

One thing I am sure of is Sin will die for this.

Blood or not, he took something that can't be given back, and he took it without remorse. He lied, covered it up and then ran like the coward he is. Sasha's spirit is broken, she's no longer the carefree version I remember, something he'll pay for. Every tear he made her shed, all the pain he caused her that day will be taken out of his flesh a piece at a time. It won't be a mercy killing. I won't put a bullet in his brain. I'll take him to hell and bring him back again. He'll plead for me to end him. He'll cry for leniency, and I won't give it.

Holding her in my arms again felt like coming home. I was able to push my own pain down, forget the shit I've seen and done over the years and stand in front of her, feeling whole for the first time in a long time. I was able to breathe again. She soothes the beast that rages inside me, quietening my mind in a way I haven't had since I last held her.

As soon as I touched her, I was certain of one thing: I'm not letting her go again.

Sasha is mine, and I'm going to make her mine again no matter what it takes. I'll do what I should have done three years ago—I'll fight for her.

Forgiveness is not something I deserve, but it's something I'm going to earn. I don't know how I can make it up to her, but I'll find a way. Killing my brother is the first step to recovery. Knowing he can never hurt her again will go some way to calming the anger that burns in my veins.

I peer down at the woman who was once my everything, wondering if she can become that again, if she'll let me make her that again. Things have changed and I don't know if we can slip back into the roles we held, but I want to. I spent three years angry at the wrong person, three years hating a woman who went through hell. That makes my anger at my brother grow. He caused that. His deception made me lose sight of the truth I always knew deep down—Sasha wouldn't have left me without a reason, and now I know that reason.

Part of me wants to pick up where we left off, but I know that can't happen. Trust has to be rebuilt, bridges that were once burnt need to be reconstructed. Can we fix this? I don't know, but I sure as fuck want to try.

Judging from her reactions, I think she does too. I don't miss how her breath hitches when she meets my gaze, or the rapid rise and fall of her chest. Eyes full of uncertainty scan my face, waiting for my next move, and I hate that I've made her unsure. I don't want her fear. I never want that, not from her.

But behind the fear is something else, something I recognise instantly. A burning desire that matches my own.

She still wants me. It might be lust, but I'll make her fall in love with me again. I let her walk away three years ago. I won't make that same mistake. Sasha is my girl, my everything.

I tuck a piece of her hair behind her ear before cupping her face and drawing her forehead to mine. The need to touch her snaps through my fingers, making me twitchy.

"I'll make this right," I pledge again, my voice raw. I mean every word of it.

But her head shakes as she blows out a shuddering breath. "You can't fix this."

She speaks the words so softly, I can barely hear her. They tear a hole in my chest that makes it difficult to draw in air. In my life, I've been captured, tortured, but nothing has ever felt as painful as those words falling from her lips.

I don't say anything else. I dip my head, bringing my mouth inches from hers, our breaths mixing.

I want to kiss her and let all my emotions bleed through

that one gesture, but she pulls away and I let her go, even though it goes against every instinct to allow it.

Our fingers slip through each other's like sand in an hourglass, and I watch as she moves to the bed, running her fingers through her daughter's hair—a daughter that could be mine.

I'm not sure how I feel about the idea of being a father, but every time I think about Lily-May being mine a surge of protectiveness scorches through me. My need to keep them both safe is on hyperdrive right now. Nothing and no one will touch them. They're mine.

With that thought, I shift my gaze to Lily-May. Daughter or niece, it doesn't matter to me. Lily-May is still blood and she's mine, just like her mother.

My anger flares as I think of Sin touching Sasha, defiling her.

As if sensing the path my thoughts have taken, Sasha says, "What happened is in the past. It needs to stay there."

I watch her gentleness with Lily-May as she strokes a finger over her chubby toddler cheek. I don't want to cut through the moment, but I shake my head.

"Wrong. You think I'm just going to roll over and let him get away with it?" I take a deep breath and try to curb all my anger for when it's needed. "This won't be buried until he is." This isn't in the past for me. It's very much our present right now, and it's consuming my every thought. "Sin isn't going to get away with what he did. He touched..." I break off, the words sticking in my throat. I still can't say it. "He hurt you. That can't go unpunished."

"He did all those things, but he did it to me, Rav. He's still your brother, the one you raised, looked after. Can you really end him? Stand in front of him and put a bullet in him? Nox should never have said anything."

I bend at the waist, so I'm at her eye level. "He stopped being family the moment he took what didn't belong to him! The moment he hurt you he knew his pathetic life was over, so yes, I can end him. I'm going to bleed him for what he's done." I grind my jaw together, speaking deathly low. "You should have told me, not Nox."

She lifts her chin and I see some of that hardness in her gaze as those walls I brought down a moment ago shoot back up.

"You wouldn't have been ready to hear it, and you not believing me would have killed me more than what that bastard did to me."

A new anger pumps through me. How can she think I would take his side? Did she not see how fucking pussy whipped I was over her back then? She walked on water for me. I fucking loved her.

I still love her, if I'm being honest.

That never changed. Even when I was pissed at her and hating her, I loved her deep down. I don't believe in fate or any of that shit, but I know she's the only woman for me. She's the only woman who could open my heart, the only one I could love.

It guts me to know she had to go through this, that she had to deal with the fallout of what Sin did alone. She'll never have to do anything by herself again. Now, she has the club—she has me.

I dip my head to meet her eyes.

"I'll have a prospect on the door within the hour."

"You're leaving?" I hate that there's fear in her voice, even though she does her best to hide it.

"I need to, sweetheart. You won't be alone."

She'll never be alone again.

With a lingering look, I step through the door. It kills me

to walk away from her, but right now I have a more important objective—finding Sin and protecting Sasha and Lily-May. Then, I can get my family back.

SASHA

MY CONVERSATION with Ravage leaves me reeling. He was angry, but beneath the anger was hurt and the old flame of desire I've dreamed of seeing again since I returned to Kessington. He wants me still, and that confuses me. How could he want someone like me? The filth that covers me will never wash off and I don't want to soil him with my dirt. Living in this world, I know there are two things capable of bringing a man like Rav to their knees—death and their woman getting hurt. He's in pain right now and it slices through my gut knowing that. I've had three years to come to terms with what happened to me. He's going to need a little time to wrap his head around it.

As I sit at my daughter's bedside, I feel numb. I don't want people to know what was done to me. I don't want people to look at me like I'm damaged goods. I don't want to see the pity in their eyes. I'm swimming in dirt and nothing will change that.

I peer at my child. The love I have for her is unrivalled by any other. I don't care how she came into this world. She's mine, and nothing changes that—not what was done to me and not the trauma of how she was created, if Sin is her father. I still hold onto the hope that she's Rav's, not because it would change anything for me, but because it would be better for her. I know with every breath in my body that he would protect her with his last breath, if he's her father. She'd have the protection of the club too. He wouldn't let anything touch her. He would slay her dragons and keep the monsters away.

Sin is the complete opposite. He made me believe I was worthless, that no one would believe me. He was wrong. So fucking wrong.

Nox and Rav both believe what happened to me and he'll get what's coming to him. I see the truth in Rav's eyes when he says he's going to make Sin pay. I fully believe he'll send Sin to hell with a smile on his face. I should feel bad about being the reason a life will have ended, but I don't. Sin took something from me I can never replace. He took my sense of security, my safety and tore it away. He made me realise I'm vulnerable, and that I can be hurt in ways so vile it leaves lasting scars that brand my soul.

I know this is hard for Rav. I can see it in his eyes. He loves his brother. He was more a father than a sibling to him growing up, so I can imagine how much this is hurting him. I hate that I inflicted that on him. For all our problems, I never wanted to hurt Rav, but I can't change what happened either. All I can do is live with it.

Having him back in my life is confusing. I don't know where I stand with him now that he knows. I do know I saw a flicker of the old Tyler behind his eyes when he held me. There was something more there that I haven't seen since I've been back. He needs me, as if I'm the balm to his tortured soul.

My feelings are a jumbled mess and I have no idea how to work through them. I don't blame his initial anger towards me. I left one day without a word or a reason. Rav puts on a front, but beneath that hardness, he's still that little kid who was betrayed by his mother, and left to fend for himself by his father. Betrayal is not something he can handle. If he trusts, he does it fully, and he trusted me, opened himself completely to me. What I did, he saw that as a disloyalty, but I can't help from being hurt by his actions. The fire he's spewed at me since I got back hasn't been easy to take, even if I understand it.

I can't help my fury towards him either.

He was the one who was supposed to know me best. He was the one who was supposed to defend me. He was my safe place. I needed him to be the strong one.

What cuts me the deepest is I would have fought for him. If things had been the other way around, I would have gone to the ends of the earth to work out why he left, but he didn't fight for me. That thought sits in my gut like a cancer, rotting everything it touches. It makes all my doubts dance to the forefront and erodes my trust in him. It makes some of Sin's words ring true. He made me feel worthless and in Rav's eyes that's what I became—another nameless face.

At least until I was in his embrace again. Then all the worries and all the anger fell silent. I felt the shift between us the moment he wrapped those strong, bulky arms around me and I forgot I was just as angry at him as he was at me. I forgot he also walked away. The world around us disappeared.

All I could think was I was finally home.

The baggage I'm dragging behind me doesn't make things easy. We can't just go back to Sasha and Tyler. We're no longer the same people. I'm not sure who he is anymore. He's different, even as he's the same. I'm a new version of the old Sasha, and I'm not sure he'll like who I've become. Half the time, I'm not sure I like who I've become.

There's no softness in me now, unless it's for my daughter. I don't know that I'm capable of letting him in, of trusting him again. We can't just pick up where we left off.

My dark tormented thoughts are scattered by a knocking on the door. I peer up at the clock and realise it's been over thirty minutes since Rav left. Thirty minutes I've been sitting with my thoughts tumbling around my head, creating new wounds and opening new hurts.

"Yeah?" I say and watch as the door opens. The prospect from the gate a few days earlier sticks his head through the frame.

"Rav sent me. I'm just outside if you need anything."

I have no intention of having the club run around after me, but it does ease some of the tension settling in my chest knowing someone here will have my back and make sure I'm safe. Not knowing where Sin is has fear clawing up my spine. I'm not sure he'd be brazen enough to come to the hospital. Then again, I never thought he'd be brazen enough to rape me in mine and Rav's home.

"Thanks, uh...?"

"Zack," he supplies.

"I'm—"

"Sasha. I remember."

I give him a half smile that doesn't reach my eyes, then return my attention to my baby. I'm grateful Lily-May slept through all of that, that she didn't need to hear any foulness. Nothing will touch her or soil her ever.

Not even the sins of my past.

RAVAGE

I don't head directly back to the clubhouse, but take a detour to Kessington's high street or what's left of it. Most of it is boarded up, but there are a few stores that still remain. The roads are busy, and I weave through the traffic, lane splitting to avoid getting stuck behind the cages.

My head is swimming with everything I've learnt. I can barely see through the film of rage that is clouding my vision. I have no idea where to start looking for my brother, but I meant it when I said I was going hunting. He's a dead man walking. This violation will not go unpunished. I'm going to bleed that little fucker dry and then I'm going to dump his body in the woods where no one will ever find him. It's better than he deserves for what he's done.

Seeing Sasha break in my arms is a sight that will haunt my steps for the rest of my life. It was more than a knife to my belly. It was an axe to my heart. For that alone, Sin will pay.

I pull my bike into a space at the side of the road, cut the engine and kick the stand down before tugging the black and white skull bandanna off my face and pulling my helmet off my head.

Dark thoughts circle my brain, dark thoughts that I never thought I'd have about my own flesh and blood. Then again, I never imagined my little brother would be capable of such a disgusting act. We walk a tightrope between shadow and darkness, but what he's done is pitch-black. He stole something that can't ever be replaced. Sasha will never be the same because of what he did to her, and knowing that burns through my veins like acid.

I hate my brother for what he's done, for putting me in this position. I don't threaten to take him to his grave lightly, but letting him get away with it isn't an option either. If I'm forced to choose between my loyalty to family or my loyalty to Sasha, I'll choose her every time. He was the one who wronged her. I don't understand how the boy I raised could do this, and that freaks me the fuck out. I thought I was good at reading people. Clearly not.

I climb off the bike and head into the nearest store, ignoring the looks directed at me. I'm used to people being wary or interested. I don't give a fuck as long as they stay out of my way.

When I step into the store, my eyes automatically scan the space for threats. There's only a middle-aged woman, who makes a dash for the exit, and the store clerk, so I move over to the kids' section.

What the hell does a kid need?

I scan the shelves, and come up empty until I hit the pyjamas section. There, I find a set of PJ's with little motorcycles on them. I grin as I pick them up, feeling the soft material between my thick calloused hands.

She would look cute as fuck in these.

I stride to the register to pay, ignoring how the cashier

peers up at me through frightened eyes and shakily puts the item through the scanner. I hand over a couple of notes and tell her to keep the change.

When I head out to my bike, I see a crowd of younger lads gathered around it, eyes wide as they coo over the chrome. I don't blame them. My bike is a thing of beauty. It's a Harley Fat Boy with a custom paint job, the Untamed Sons insignia painted on the fuel tank. The rims glimmer in the sunshine as I approach and they part like the Red Sea to let me through.

"Nice bike," one of them, a teen with dark hair and glasses, gets up the courage to yell out. I can tell with a look that not one of them would survive an hour in my club.

Ignoring him, I put my bag from the store into the saddle bag on the back and pull my helmet on. I tug up the bandanna from around my neck, covering my nose and mouth before I throw my leg over the bike. The roar of the Harley pipes are loud in the quiet of the street and the lads let out a "Whoa!" as I kick the stand up and move out of the space. Then I take off up the street without a second glance back.

I ride to the clubhouse and park in my usual space next to the side doors. The change in lighting as I step inside the building has me momentarily squinting until my sight adjusts. I find the common room is busy as usual, even though it's not even noon yet. I ignore my brothers and the club bunnies, seeking Fury out like a heat-seeking missile.

My sergeant-at-arms is sitting in a booth on his own, his dark hair is loose around his face, making him look a little wild. He's playing with a knife, stabbing it between his fingers, going closer to his flesh each time. Crazy bastard.

He peers up at me as I approach, his eyebrows drawing together.

"Prez?" There's question in his voice, and I'm not surprised it's there. I'm walking a knife edge at the moment and I'm sure I'm channelling that rage physically.

"Sin's gone. I need to know who the fuck was on the gate when he left."

"On it," he assures me, standing. His knife disappears under his kutte.

"Do it fast."

He doesn't question why, just nods. I head for the bar and beckon Kyle over with two fingers. The prospect moves towards me, jutting his chin in question.

I hand over the bag with a list of instructions to make sure it gets to Sasha and Lily-May. I then tell him to order food for her from her favourite takeout place. At least, it was her favourite three years ago. When I had her in my arms, I noticed how underweight she is. I need to rebuild those curves and get my woman healthy again.

For too long, she's had to take care of everything alone. Not anymore. It's my turn to take care of her. I want to make sure nothing touches her.

When I'm sure he understands, I head for my office. As soon as the door is shut behind me, I sag against it. I know what I have to do and I know why, but that doesn't mean the weight of it isn't sitting in my gut like a wrecking ball. I don't care about putting another black mark to my name. I already have plenty, but killing Sin will take a piece of me I can't put back.

It has to be done, though.

He can't be allowed to live.

He signed his life away the moment he touched Sasha against her will.

Just as I sink down onto my seat, there's a knock on my door. I think about ignoring it, but I don't have that luxury as president of this group of misfits. It could be important.

"What?" I demand, and glance up as the door opens.

Nox steps inside and shuts the door behind him. His eyes scan my face, as if looking to see if my demons are out to play. I see the relief in them when he realises I'm not in danger of going nuclear.

"You spoke to Sash."

It's not a question, but I answer it anyway.

"Yeah," I confirm.

"And?"

"And now my brother has to die."

Nox nods, taking this information in as if I'm talking about the weather and not bleeding and killing my only remaining blood family.

"I've had feelers out all day, trying to work out where the little bastard went."

"Any luck?"

"Not yet, but he can't have gone far."

If he has any sense he will have fled to the furthest reaches of the world. Even then, I'll still find him and drag his arse home.

"She alone?" Nox asks and jealousy briefly rears its ugly head at his words. She's my girl, my problem to worry about.

"There's a prospect with them."

Zack better protect Sasha and Lily-May with his last dying fucking breath. I'll gut him myself if anything happens to them.

"If you need to be with them—"

"I need to find Sin first. Make sure everyone knows Sash and Lily-May are under my protection."

Nox cocks his head to one side, his eyes boring holes into me. He doesn't interrogate me, as I expect. Instead, he just says, "You've got it."

Some of the tension in my chest eases a little at his agreement.

I'm going to find my brother, kill him, and make the world a little safer for my girls, but first, I have to find him.

SASHA

"JUST TRY TO EAT SOMETHING, BABY," I try to cajole my daughter with a bowl of porridge, but she shakes her head stubbornly and then sobs, her little fists rubbing at her eyes in a way that pierces my heart. I hate seeing her like this, suffering so much she can't even eat without feeling sick or in pain.

Placing the bowl on the bedside cabinet, I run a hand over her head before pressing my lips to her hair. She's tearing me apart and I don't know how to make things better for her.

"Maybe try again later," Jessa, the nurse standing at the side of the bed, says as she adds more painkillers to her drip, sympathy playing across her face.

I give her a small smile that I don't feel. I don't need her sympathy. Lil is my daughter. I should be able to give her what she needs and the helplessness that washes through me that I can't shreds what is left of my strength.

I wait until Jessa leaves the room, then I break down. I move to the window, giving Lily my back so she can't see my tears, my arms wrapping around my middle. I can't do this anymore. I can't deal with my daughter being sick and my secret being out. It's all too much. I'm too exposed, everything feels too raw.

Swiping angrily at my wet face, I turn back to the bed and peer at the little girl who needs me to be strong, and that gives me the strength to shut my emotions down. I have to do this for her.

The test will be back tomorrow and then we'll know if she has a chance. I'm holding out hope Rav will be a match. Getting Sin tested is not an option now, not that I think he'd be selfless enough to do it anyway, but Rav will kill him the moment he sets eyes on him.

Pain slices through my chest as I try not to think about the possibility that Rav's test might not come back positive. If it doesn't, I don't know what I'll do. It isn't the end of the line for Lily-May, but it's pretty close to it.

There's a knock on the door and I quickly wipe my tears away before saying come in.

Zack steps into the room holding a couple of packages.

"This just came for you."

My brow draws together as confusion settles over me. "For me?"

"Yeah. From Rav."

My eyes dart to his face before coming to the bags he's holding. He places them on the table and gives me a smile. "If you need anything…"

His words disperse some of the pain in my chest.

"I'll let you know."

I wait until he's gone to open the first bag. Inside, I find two tubs of what looks like Chinese food. I tug off the lid and realise it's my favourite dish. Three years later and he still remembers. My heart gallops in my chest as I stare down at the vegetable Chow Mein, the delicious scents wafting up and making my mouth water. I can't believe he did this for me.

I put the lid back on and open the second bag. I pull out a pair of pyjamas identical to the pair I bought Lily-May myself. These are in pale green rather than white and have little motorcycles on them. I can tell by looking they're going to be too big, but seeing this makes my eyes fill with tears again. I dip back into the bag and pull out another garment. This one is a white tee with the club's insignia—a crowned skull with wings—on it and the words 'biker in training' on the back. My hand flies to my mouth as I try to calm the ache in my chest. It's an acceptance of me, of Lily-May. Rav's never been good with words, but these things say more than his words ever could. He's trying to take care of us. I can't help the smile that graces my lips as I fold the clothes and place them in the locker at the side of the bed, then open the vegetable Chow Mein again. It's still warm and I'm starving. I can't remember the last time I ate something that didn't come out of a vending machine or the hospital canteen.

The first mouthful has me moaning as the spices and sweetness explode over my tongue. It's been too long since I last had this and it tastes as good as I remember. It's also been too long since I last ate properly.

"Mummy. Food for me."

I look up to see Lily-May's wide eyes staring at my food.

I hand her a piece of carrot and instead of her nose scrunching up, she nibbles on it.

When she's finished with the carrot, I give her another piece, and she takes it, sucking it between her lips, a smile dancing on her face.

She holds out a sticky hand.

"More."

I can't help but laugh. Relief that she's finally eating makes me a little giddy.

"You like that, huh?"

She nods and I swear in that moment I'll get this dish for

her every day, so long as she's eating.

We demolish the food, barely coming up for air between bites. Then I clean her hands and change her into the PJ's Rav sent for her. They're a little baggy, as I expected, but she still looks adorable.

Lily-May settles down, dozing in and out, her full belly making her sleepy.

I sit back in the chair at the side of the bed, a small smile gracing my lips.

I never thought I'd see a glimpse of the old Rav—the old Tyler—but his actions tell me he wants to make amends, and I want to let him. I've missed him in my life. I loved him. I still do. That's never changed. Being without him was a torture I struggled to endure. Without Lily-May to focus on I'm not sure I would have survived.

I don't know how we go back to who we were, though. Things have transformed so much. Neither of us are the same people anymore. We're both changed by what's happened.

I sit with Lily-May for an hour or two as she sleeps, my thoughts on what Rav did for us. The tee might seem like just a tee to an outsider, but I see it for what it is. It's Rav claiming Lily-May in the eyes of the club. Knowing she'll have his protection settles me, makes the demons subside a little and lets me breathe easier for the first time in years.

I hear a ruckus outside the room and my feet move before I consider my own safety. I tug it open and see the corridor is filled with bikers, the Untamed Sons' insignia of wings behind a crowned skull staring back at me. My stomach flips and fear shrouds me. What the fuck is happening?

Nox spots me and pushes through the group to come to me.

"What's going on?" I demand, my eyes sliding past him. It looks like the entire club emptied out, old ladies, including the club bunnies, and Titch's ex-wife, Rachel. I'm surprised she came. They had two boys right out of high school and got married as soon as they turned eighteen. The marriage didn't last long, though.

"We're trying to get the bitch on the desk to let us take the test."

"The test?" I hold my breath as I wait for his answer.

"The one your kid needs."

Tears prick my eyes and I force them not to fall. I won't break down in front of Nox again, even though I want to.

"Nox…"

"It was Rav's idea," he says.

I peer around the group and see familiar faces from another lifetime ago. Daimon, Fury, Titch, Whizz. The rest I don't recognise. They must have patched in after I left.

Daimon smirks at me, his dark hair dripping into his eyes as he tips his head forward. He makes the first move, gesturing for me to come to him.

My feet go before I consider what I'm doing and then I'm wrapped in his arms, smelling the scent of leather and cigarettes—a scent that is all Daimon.

I'm passed to Titch who squeezes me so tightly my ribs feel like they might break before Whizz has his turn. I pause at Fury, not sure what to do. The man doesn't like being touched.

His brows draw together as he says, "You look different."

A smile graces my lips. "You too, Fury."

This right here is what I've been missing these past few years. Family. This is my family, and they're all here for me and Lily-May. A lump settles in my throat as I raise my gaze towards Nox who is peering at me with soft eyes.

I don't know how the fuck I walked away from them. I'll never do it again. No one will ever convince me my place isn't right here.

RAVAGE

THE NEXT MORNING, I head to the hospital early. We're due to get the results back from my test. I'm on edge to find out if I'm a match. Fuck, I've never prayed before, but last night I got down on my knees and asked for help for Lily-May.

I want to see Sash before the results, so I get there a little before the appointment.

I don't bother to knock on the room door, and when I push inside I find Sasha propped up in a chair at the side of the bed, her head tipped onto her upturned palm, her eyes closed.

My mouth pulls down into a line, an ache festering in my belly. When was the last time she slept? When was the last time she had five minutes to herself? I know she's worried about Lily-May, but the black smudges under her eyes show me how tired she is, how much this is taking its toll on her.

I shouldn't do it, but I can't stop myself. I seize the opportunity and move over to the cot bed to peer down at Lily-May. She's asleep, her head turned to the side, her thumb sticking out of her mouth. My lips turn up at the corners and I feel a hint of pride when I see she's wearing the pyjamas I bought her. They're hanging off her, a size too big, but they're still cute as fuck, even with the wires snaking out from underneath them. Sasha putting them on her is an acceptance of me coming into their lives.

I stare at the baby, my mind a maelstrom of motion. As I look at her, I know she's mine. I don't know how, but I just know I'm her father, and not because I've claimed them both, but just because I feel this connection with Lily-May that goes beyond loving her because she's Sasha's. I've learnt over the years to trust my gut, and right now I trust what my gut is telling me.

I'm her father, no matter what some DNA test says.

I should be scared, but I'm not. I'm ready for this new challenge. I always wanted a family. Family has always been an important part of my identity, probably because mine was such a clusterfuck when I was younger. My father, who died when I was nineteen, was mostly absent in my life, too wrapped up in the club to notice his sons were drowning, and I haven't seen my crack addict mother since Dad brought us to live with him. I created my own family, which is why Sin's betrayal cuts deeply. He didn't consider those bonds important when he attacked and hurt Sasha.

It makes me want that paternity test even more. Not for my peace of mind, but for Sasha's. A paternity test might clear out some of the monsters chasing on her heels.

"What…?" Her sleepy voice has me glancing over my shoulder. Sasha is straightening in her seat, rubbing at her eyes, her movements slow. When she sees me, her brows draw together. "Rav?"

"I didn't mean to wake you."

She rubs at her neck and I expect to see wariness in her eyes, but that's not what I get. There's softness and need as she takes me in, and I want to see more of that.

"It's okay," she assures me, pushing up from the chair and

coming to the cot bed. Her jeans are those skin-tight type that hug her figure, showing me just how much weight she's lost. It has my teeth gritting. She needs to take better care of herself.

Sasha glances down at Lily-May, her expression becoming more tender. Then she does what I wanted to do and reaches out to run a hand over her hair.

"You're here for the test results?" she asks, splitting her gaze between me and Lily-May.

"Yeah."

Her eyes shift to the clock on the wall. "The doctor isn't seeing us until after nine-thirty."

"I know," I tell her and I watch her eyes soften as she realises I came early out of choice.

"Thank you—for yesterday. The clothes, the food. Lily-May ate for the first time in days."

Her smile slays me and I vow to make her do it every fucking day from now on.

"That's good to hear, sweetheart."

"And thanks for getting all the guys here, too. It meant a lot to me and Lil."

"They wanted to come." It's not a lie. When I told them what was going on, they all volunteered to do the test. They don't know what happened between Sin and Sasha—only Nox knows this—and I don't plan on telling anyone either. Sasha shouldn't have to live with this shit trailing behind her.

"Even Fury came."

I trace her face, committing every inch of it to memory. God, she's beautiful. How did I go so long without her?

"Yeah. He wanted to."

Fury hates hospitals and anything that might involve needles. The last time he needed a blood test, it took three of the guys to hold him down, so Whizz could get it from him.

He still managed to cause a few black eyes. I was surprised he wanted to come down and take the test at all, but that crazy fucker was insistent. He always did have a soft spot for Sash. Thank fuck it was only a swab test.

She stares at me for a moment, and I wonder what is going through that head of hers. Then she says, "You don't have to look after us."

"Yeah, babe, I do."

My gaze tracks her tongue as it dips out to wet her bottom lip before she tucks her hair behind her ears.

"We're not your problem."

I step into her space, forcing her head to tip back, so she can meet my eyes. I caress her cheek, relishing the feel of her soft skin beneath my rough fingers.

"We both know that's not true."

"Rav—"

"Don't argue with me, woman. You and that kid are mine and that makes your shit my shit."

She nibbles at her bottom lip and my mouth goes Sahara-dry. Does she know what she does to me?

"We can't just pick up where we left off."

"I know."

"I'm not the same person I was back then. Neither are you."

"I know that too."

I watch as she huffs out a low breath, her fingers raking through her hair. I wish it was my hands, my fingers. "I need time to digest this shit."

"You can have all the time you want, but it ain't going to make any difference. You're mine. Both of you."

She needs to realise I'm not going anywhere. I won't leave her to deal with this shit alone. Not this time, but if she needs to feel in control, I'll give her that. I'll give her anything she fucking wants. I have three years to make up for. It gores me knowing that I'm the one who has caused that hesitancy in her eyes, that uncertainty that I hate seeing. I don't know how I break through her walls, but I'll find a way because I won't let her walk away again.

She peers up at me and I want to take her mouth, claim her, show her who she belongs to, but I don't. She's not ready to go there—yet.

When she is, I'll be waiting.

"What about the paternity test?" I ask, needing to know.

Just like that her smile is wiped off her face. I hate that desolate look in her eyes as memories plague her, but it has to be done. She needs to know Lily-May is mine for sure. It's the only way to lay her demons to rest. Not knowing is slowly killing her piece by piece.

When she doesn't answer, I add, "I know why you don't want to do one, but I know she's mine."

It's selfish as fuck to push her for this, but she needs it. We both do.

"You can't know that." Her voice comes out little more than a whisper.

I thump my chest. "I feel it in here. She's fucking mine."

"If you think that then why do it?" Her anger flares as her emotions overwhelm her. I can see the tight lines of her body as she fists her hands at her sides, trying and failing to maintain control.

"Because you need to have closure."

My strong girl is struggling to keep a grip here and I trail my fingers down her cheek.

She peers up at me, her teeth gritting. "I don't care who her father is."

I don't believe that for a second.

"Yeah, you do, sweetheart. Just think about it."

I can see the cogs working in her brain as she nods. My thoughts scatter as there's a knock on the door. A nurse pushes into the room, her expression filled with apology.

"The doctor's ready to see you now."

My gut rolls. Time to find out if I can save Lily-May's life.

18

SASHA

THE WALK down the corridor to the doctor's office feels like I'm taking the green mile to the execution chamber. My steps falter and if it wasn't for Rav steadying me, I would fold like wet cardboard. My pulse is galloping, my mouth is dry and my head is dizzied.

As soon as we step into the room, I know bad news is coming. I can see it in the tight set of Dr Harking's shoulders, the sadness clouding his eyes, as he waits for us to take our seats in front of his desk. My neck feels hot, clammy and my stomach starts to churn as icy fingers twist my gut.

Rav's fingers curl around mine as we take a seat in the two chairs in front of the desk, his calloused palms scraping over mine. I squeeze his hand back, trying to communicate what I can't say in words—that I'm grateful for him being here. And I am. His touch grounds me, keeps my feet rooted to the floor as my world readies itself for the bottom to fall out of it again.

I watch the doctor steel himself, then he delivers the crushing blow. "I'm sorry to say, you're not a full match, Mr Jenkins."

Dr Harking's words stab at my chest, making it hard to draw air past the lump in my throat. Lily-May's last chance of survival is going up in flames and I can hardly breathe. Every inhalation is more painful than the last. All this heartache, reliving the painful steps of my past, of facing my rapist and chasing my demons has been for nothing.

Rav isn't a match.

My hand covers my mouth as bile races up my throat. This can't be happening. I lean forward in the chair, trying to drag in a lungful of air and failing. Rav's hand goes to the back of my neck, squeezing tightly, trying to assure me he's here. I suck in a breath, feeling light-headed.

"Please, don't feel like everything is lost," the doctor says. "We still have the results to come through from your friends. Perhaps one of them will match fully. If not, we're still searching the national database. People are added to it every day. There's still also the option to use a partial match from you or Mr Jenkins."

I'm going to vomit.

I take a deep gulp of air in and try to control my stomach, which is roiling viciously. My skin crawls, a trail of fire licking its way over me. I scrub at my arms, trying to stop the sensation, but it doesn't help.

"I'll give you both a moment," the doctor finally says, as if sensing his presence is intruding on a deeply personal moment.

I hear the door snick shut behind me and then I lose it. Tears brim in my eyes before spilling down my cheeks. I try to hold back a sob, but it rips out of me. It sounds loud in the silence of the room.

"Fuck," Rav yells.

I peer up at him. His face is a pale mask of anger and I can see he's barely keeping his shit together. His fists clench and unclench at his side, itching to take the rage building in him out on something physically. He's holding on by a thread, I can see it, but I see the strength there too as he tries to keep it together to help me.

He moves in front of the chair, crouching in front of me. His hands lock around mine.

"I'll fix this," he promises me.

"How?"

"I'll fucking fix it," he repeats, as if there's no option but to make this right.

"How!" I scream in his face, sobbing as I do.

He grabs my cheeks and his touch brings me back to reality for a moment. Then he pulls me against his chest. I go willingly, unable to stop my tears.

"I'll find a way to make this better."

I cling to his kutte, my knuckles whitening. "This was her last chance. She's so tired, Rav."

I watch as he flinches away from my words, as if he's been physically punched in the gut. He shakes his head, denial written in every line of his face.

"I just got you both back. I'm not losing—" He cuts himself off.

Something the doctor said, suddenly pricks at the back of my mind. He said he's not a *full* match.

I grab at Rav.

"Get the doctor back."

"Babe…"

I push up and shove past him to the door, dragging it open. Dr Harking is standing at the nurses' station and glances up as the door opens. I move to him, Rav on my heels.

"You said he wasn't a full match."

"Both parents are always at least half matches. They carry four out of eight markers needed to be considered for a successful transplant. Our hope was that Mr Jenkins would be a full match, not a half. We can transplant marrow from either you or Mr Jenkins, but as I've told you before there are risks with a partial match. There's an increased chance the marrow won't engraft and there's potential for infection afterwards. It's better to have a full match, which is what we'll look for, but if necessary, we can transplant from either of you."

I ignore everything he said, but the first part. I know it by heart. I've heard it a thousand times. I've read every piece of information out there on my daughter's condition.

Hope surges in me as I dare to ask, "Both parents?" I hold my breath. "Rav—Mr Jenkins—is her father?"

The doctor's brows draw together as his eyes dart between us, sensing he's stumbled into something more here. "Biological parents are always a half match to their children. He half matched... but I can't say for sure he's her father."

My breath catches in my throat. It's good enough for me, and I want to believe it so badly. I need to believe it. I spin to Rav, grabbing his biceps and clinging to him with a desperation that catches me off guard.

"You're her father." My lip quivers as tears stream down my cheeks.

He peers down at me and I see the tears shimmering in his own eyes. "I told you that."

"But it's official. You couldn't share those markers if you weren't. Biological parents have half the markers. You're her daddy."

I'm grasping at straws, but I don't care. It might be coincidence he shares those markers. It might mean something else, but I take a full breath for the first time in minutes, gulping down air like a thirsty survivor of a drought.

"He said possibly, not definitely. I still want that test, Sash. You need to know for sure."

The weight in my chest has eased, allowing me to breathe

freely for the first time in years. It's the closest I have to proof Rav is her father and I cling to it fiercely.

"Okay."

He pulls me into his arms, squeezing me, his hand going to the back of my neck, collaring my nape.

"I'll make this right," he tells me, and I'm not sure if he's talking about Lily-May, Sin or both.

He dips his head and presses his mouth to mine. I forget about the doctor, the nurses, that we're in a public corridor. All my thoughts are locked on the strong man holding me and taking me, a man who was once my everything, a man I wish would become that again.

Forgiveness isn't something that comes easily to me, but I also can't be angry at Rav forever. He didn't know the full story about why I left. He had every right to be pissed. Since he found out what Sin did to me, he's gone out of his way to be here for me and Lily-May. Because of that I find my resolve to keep away from him weakening. Even if I wanted him out of my life, I know he'd never go—not now. Lily-May is his, and he'll never walk away from his child.

His mouth moves over mine, taking, devouring me as if I'm his reason for breathing, and I let him. I need this. I need him. My legs feel shaky as he presses his body against mine, my heart fluttering wildly in my chest. This is the Rav I remember. The Rav I fell in love with. My Tyler.

When he pulls back, he's breathless, but so am I. Dazed, I peer up at him, blinking to clear my dizzied vision.

"Rav…"

"Ty, baby. You call me Ty."

My heart soars at this. It's an acceptance, one I've been desperately craving. It feels like a win in a game I'm stacked to lose.

"Tyler," I try his name on my tongue, liking how it feels, watching the effect it has over him.

The doctor clears his throat, and I put a hand on Ty's arm as he steps towards him menacingly. He stops, just about.

"I've put a rush on the other results. Please, be prepared the news might not be what you hope for. There's a very slim chance of a stranger being a match, one in a million, though it does happen."

Glacial cold sweeps through my belly at his words.

"If we can't find a match?" Ty asks.

"Then we have to risk the half-match, taking bone marrow from you or Miss Montgomery. As I mentioned, this is risky, but it's the only choice we might have."

I knew that could be an option. It was why I went to find Ty and Sin. I've read everything there is to read on this disease and its treatment and I knew there was a slim chance one of them could match her more closely than me, though it was more likely they would also be a half match. A slim chance was better than no chance and I'd do anything to give Lily-May the best opportunity of survival, including pulling all my demons out of the closet for the world to see.

"All we can do is wait for the other tests to come back and see where we go from there," the doctor tells us.

"Thank you."

Ty pulls me away from the desk and into a corner of the corridor.

"There's still hope," he tells me and I rake my fingers through my hair, quiet desperation making my movements jerky.

"Taking from me or you isn't ideal. It reduces the chances of the transplant taking."

"But it's still an option." He kisses me. "That's all she needs—options."

I lean my head against his chest, gripping the lapels of his kutte. "Thank you, for being here today. I don't think I could have got through this alone."

"You'll never be alone again, Sash."

His words warm me and I peer up at him. "You're her father."

"She was mine anyway, I told you this."

"She's not Sin's." I let my tears fall, relief making my walls tumble. "She can't be if you are compatible with her. Parents always have half of the markers of the child."

I'm rambling, but I don't care. I feel like the world has been lifted off my back, letting me stand straight for the first time in years.

"You're both mine, and I'm going to spend however long it takes showing you that."

19

RAVAGE

I PAY a small fortune to a private lab on the other side of London to do the paternity test. They can have the results back in a week, which is the reason I chose them. I don't want Sasha waiting longer than she has to. She needs this issue put to bed, and fast. The relief in her when she thought I was Lily-May's father cut a hole in my chest and tore out my heart. She needs to know for sure. It's the only way she can heal and start to rebuild her life.

I don't need the test to know the truth. Lily-May is mine. I feel it in my bones. I want Sasha to be sure, though. She needs this closure. Even if the test says I'm not, which I doubt, I am this child's father. I'll raise her as mine. She'll never know the truth of how she came into this world.

One look at that little girl and I was smitten. She fills a place in my heart I didn't know needed filling, but it seems like it was reserved for her. Even so, I can't help but feel I fell at the first hurdle—saving my daughter's life. I needed that bone marrow test to match me. Being only a partial match is no use to my child. It shreds me that I can't be the one to ride in and save the day, prove I'm worthy of this little girl who has already claimed me. I just fucking pray one of my brothers will be the one in a million the doctor said we need. They have to be, because Lily-May's chance of survival diminishes if we can't find a full match. Sasha leaving me changed me in ways I can never fix, but losing my daughter will bring me to my knees.

It's early when I walk through the common room. The quiet is the opposite of the normal chaos that exists here. It's not empty, though. On one of the sofas, I see Levi is asleep, a body lying on top of him. The swath of blonde hair tells me it's most likely Noelle. She's wearing just a thong, the globes of her arse cheeks sticking up like two voluminous round mountains, and her bare breasts are pressed against his chest. Neither of them stir as I cross the floor to the bar and move around the back of it. I grab a soft drink from the fridge, opening it and swigging back a mouthful.

I want to get back to the hospital as soon as possible this morning. I tried to convince Sasha to leave last night, to get some rest and eat properly, but she refused, and I don't want to push her yet. Every day she opens herself more and more to me and the trust between us is growing again.

I wouldn't have left her, but I still have hunting to do. I still have to find my fucking brother. He continues to evade us, which makes my gut churn with fire. I need him found. I need to put an end to the mess he created. Sasha will be able to breathe a little easier with him gone.

I didn't leave Sasha alone at the hospital. Kyle is with her and her friend, Lucy, is there too. I've made sure she has a constant stream of brothers, just in case Sin decides to show up. I don't think he'd have the balls, but who knows where his head is at right now. I'm not willing to risk Sasha and Lily-May's safety.

I hear the door open and glance up as Fury strides in, clutching Zack by the back of his kutte.

I see the demons rising in his eyes as he readies himself for whatever action I demand and I don't miss the blade he's clutching in his right hand, ready to slide into the prospect if I say so. His eyes are a little crazy this morning, and the bags under them make me wonder if he's been to sleep yet.

As Fury stops in front of me, he doesn't say a word, just stares at me. The steadily forming bruises and blood dripping from his nose tells me Fury has already let some of his pent-up energy out on Zack and is waiting for confirmation he can inflict more damage.

I break the stalemate. "He's who let Sin out of the compound?"

Fury nods.

I place my coke bottle on the top of the bar, then ram my balled-up fist into Zack's gut hard enough to lift him off his feet.

He doubles over, gasping for breath, holding himself around the middle as he tries to draw air into his lungs.

He doesn't try to defend himself or explain. Like a good little soldier, he doesn't make up any fucking excuses for what he did, but I want an explanation from him. I want to know why he allowed my brother to gain freedom, putting Sasha and my daughter at risk.

"Why?" I hiss out.

"No one said he couldn't leave," Zack swallows, his Adam's apple bobbing and I'm impressed at his backbone as he faces me off. I don't need shrinking violets in my club. I need strong brothers who I know will always have my back. "He's a patched brother."

"*Was* a patched brother," I correct, letting go of some of my anger.

I fucked up here, not Zack. He's done everything he's been taught to do, and has even taken a beating for it. He couldn't have questioned Sin. His place is below a patched brother. My fuck up was not telling anyone Sin wasn't allowed to leave. That shit lands on my door, but my head had been a mess after Sasha dropped the bomb about my brother.

"He doesn't get through the gate again, you hear me?"

"Yeah, Rav, I hear."

I turn to Fury. "Make sure everyone knows, including the prospects. Fuck, even the club bunnies. Tell everyone."

He nods. I grab my coke off the top of the bar and take a swig as Fury gives Zack a shove towards the door. The prospect stumbles before he rights himself and makes a quick dash for the exit. I can see the disappointment in Fury's eyes as his knife disappears under his kutte.

Crazy bastard.

I slide my half empty bottle on the counter and push away. "I'm heading to the hospital. Anything happens here, call me."

I'm trying not to let things slide in the club. It will always be my priority, but my focus is locked on my woman and kid. I need my brothers to pick up my slack while I'm sorting shit out.

"We'll take care of shit," Fury assures me.

I don't doubt that, but his idea of taking care of anything usually ends with bloodshed.

As I step into the corridor, I see Nox coming towards the common room.

"Any luck finding Sin yet?" I ask.

He shakes his head. "Little fucker is good at hiding."

He would be. I taught him everything he knows. Frustration gnaws at my gut. I need him found. I need to make this problem disappear. "I want the whole club on this. Sasha and Lily-May aren't safe while he's out there."

"We'll find him," he assures me, but tingles still race up

my spine and a sour feeling settles in my gut. I hate not knowing where he is.

"Quickly, Nox. Check all our warehouses and any abandoned properties we have. Put the feelers out there. Someone has got to know something."

The longer he's out there, the more I feel a noose tighten around my throat.

"How's Sash?"

"She's keeping it together."

He peers at me for a moment, before he says, "If she and the kid need anything…"

"Thanks. I'm going to put it forward officially in church tomorrow, but I want you to step up as VP. With Sin out of the picture I need a right-hand man I can trust."

His eyes flare with shock before he regains control of his emotions. "Whatever you need, Rav."

What I need is my brother found and this mess to be over with. Killing Sin won't be easy, as much as I'm trying to convince myself it will. The thought of harming him conflicts with all my years of keeping him safe.

Doing this will stain my soul so black I'm not sure I'll be able to come back from it, but it has to be done. I can't allow a rapist piece of shit to walk free. I can't allow him to have hurt Sasha and do nothing. I'll look him in the eyes as I drag the knife through his flesh and I'll make him suffer because that's what he did to my girl. He took her dignity, her control and he can't ever give that back. Killing him is the only choice I have, but that doesn't mean it won't taint me.

Sin was the only blood family I ever cared about, at least until I found out about Lily-May. Dad's gone, Mum's in the wind. The only family we ever had growing up was the club and each other. That he put me in this position burns like hot embers in my belly, but I can't look at him without feeling hate and disgust. We could never go back to the way things were. I couldn't live with him breathing the same air as Sasha and my daughter.

So, he has to die.

"When we were kids, before we went to live with my father, we'd sleep down by the railway tracks sometimes."

Nox bobs his head. "I'll head down there and see if he's been seen."

"Make sure you recover his kutte."

"Yeah."

I head out to my bike, thoughts colliding around my brain and climb on. Then I make my way to the hospital to see my girls.

20

SASHA

LILY-MAY SLEEPS most of the morning, but she wakes up crying and I can't do anything to settle her. The nurse gives her more pain medication, but it doesn't work either. My heart feels like it's tearing open as her cries pierce my ears. I'm exhausted, mentally and physically drained. I don't know how much longer I can keep being strong. I'm falling apart at the seams.

Lucy tries to settle her too, but nothing is working. She fusses, her little fingers curled into fists as she tries to deal with her pain. My tears flow freely as I watch my child suffering and am helpless to stop it. I would take all her pain for her if I could. I would take it a thousand times over.

I swipe my tears away as I run my hand over her hair, trying to soothe her. It takes her a while, but she does eventually drift off. I breathe easier as her own breaths become slower and steadier.

The door opens and I twist to see Tyler standing in the doorway, his kutte on his back as always, the dark blue shirt he's wearing straining beneath the thick cut of his muscles. I smile, but I know it doesn't reach my eyes, which are still watering.

"What's wrong?" he demands immediately.

Lucy speaks before I can. "Lily-May's having a bad morning."

I watch Ty's jaw tighten at this news, watch the darkness cloud his eyes as he strides towards the cot bed. His hand reaches out, as if he wants to touch her. He's hesitant, and I hate that he is. He should feel comfortable touching his own child.

"It's okay," I tell him, my voice dropping low.

He runs a hand over her hair and my heart breaks for him. He should have been with his daughter from her first breath. I denied him that.

For a moment, he just keeps stroking her hair, his eyes locked on her like she's the most precious thing on earth and I watch in silence, letting him have this moment with Lily-May who seems to settle more under his hand.

Lucy glances at me to make sure I'm okay with him being here. I nod and she eyes him before she slips from the room, giving us the privacy we need.

Tyler's eyes roam over our daughter, his brow knitting together. I can see him trying to work out how to make this right. There is no making this right, though. Helplessness washes through me like poisonous acid, corroding my veins.

"What does she need?"

"The transplant." I rake my fingers through my hair, trying to calm my breathing. I feel short of breath, on edge and terrified. I don't want to lose my daughter. Not after such a short time with her. I want to see her marry, grow older, have children of her own, if that's possible after the transplant. I want to be in her life until I take my last breath.

"If I have to call in all the chapters of the Sons to do the test, I'll do it. We'll get her this match," Ty assures me.

I draw air in shakily and peer up at him. He's so confident he can fix this, can make it better. I want to believe him, I really do, but I don't know if I can. This isn't something he can throw anger at and make right by bossing people around. This is in the hands of a higher power, one neither of us can control.

He takes my hands in his.

"We have to fight for her."

"I know."

He dips his head and takes my mouth, claiming me, marking me as he nips my bottom lip. It's a kiss that makes my knees tremble and my body feel weak. He always did have the ability to shake my foundations. I cling to him, like he's the only thing keeping me upright and when his hand collars the back of my throat, I can't help but press against his hard, lean body and want more of him.

When he breaks the kiss, I'm reluctant to let him, but he pulls back, his eyes scanning my face. His expression is a mask of anxiety that kicks me in my gut.

"We'll get through this," he tells me.

I want to believe him desperately, but months of fighting my concerns, of pushing down my fears are catching up with me. Coupled with telling my secret, I'm struggling to keep my walls up.

I'm losing my daughter with each day that passes. The disease continues to ravage her, to chip away at her strength, her resolve to keep fighting.

I can't bear it.

I cling to Tyler's kutte, smelling the leather and his after-shave, my head resting against his chest and sob as his arms wrap around me. I take strength from his grip on me, even as my heart feels like it's shattering into a million pieces. My daughter has to survive this. There's no alternative. I won't let there be.

"Don't cry, baby," he tells me, but I can't stop my tears. They fall thick and fast down my cheeks. I let him hold me, soothe my pain. I'm falling apart.

"I'm trying to be strong," I say, my fragile walls tumbling down around my head.

"You don't have to be strong anymore. I'll be strong for the three of us."

A knock on the door breaks through the moment, and I swipe quickly at my face as it opens to reveal Dr Harking. The smile on his face instantly has my spine snapping straight.

"What? What is it?" I ask.

"I rushed the results through from your friends." He grins. "We found a match."

My heart jolts beneath my ribs and the ground beneath my feet shifts. "You did?" I breathe out the words, hardly daring to believe him.

"Yes, I was astounded myself, but it's a good match with your daughter. If we transplant, it should take well."

"Who?" Ty demands.

"Uh," he glances down and flicks through the notes he's holding, "a Mr Joseph Henry."

It takes me a second to recall from his prospecting days, but I remember Joey is Fury's real name. It has to be him.

"One in a million," Tyler mutters under his breath.

I snap my gaze towards Ty. "We have a match." My voice is pitched higher than usual.

"I know."

"Lily-May will get better."

"Yeah, darlin', she will."

Relief floods me at the realisation my daughter has a chance now. She might just survive this. I send a thank you to the universe. Tingles dance in my stomach as excitement starts to bloom. I never thought we'd get a match, let alone in someone close to home. Fury's family. He didn't grow up in the club like I did, but he became family the moment he got his full colours.

"He's going to need injections, needles," I tell Ty, worry bleeding into my voice. I know how scared he is of needles.

"I know."

"Is he going to be able to do it?"

He kisses my forehead. "He wouldn't have volunteered to do the test if he wasn't going to follow through. All the guys knew there would be a chance they'd get called up."

"This is great news," Dr Harking says. "If we can get Mr Henry back in as soon as possible we can get the ball rolling and get Lily-May on the road to recovery. It's still not without risks, but the likelihood she'll take the marrow without rejecting it is greatly increased with a true match."

"Thank you so much, Doctor."

He inclines his head. "I want to see Lily-May get well, too. I'll leave you both alone."

I turn to Tyler, unable to stop my smile. "We have a match. Lily-May is going to survive."

Those words ease some of the tension in my chest, because now I know my daughter has a real shot at survival, and that's the best feeling in the world.

21

RAVAGE

THE SMILE on Sasha's face nearly breaks me. Since we found out Fury is a match for Lily-May, she hasn't stopped grinning. I watch her with our daughter, my heart feeling lighter than it has in years. I'm stained black, my soul so dark now I can never come back from it. You don't live a life like I've lived and not have that shit embedded in you, but Lily-May makes me feel like I could clean some of the dirt away. She's the only thing in my life that I've done right.

I stand at Sasha's back, rubbing circles low on her spine as she plays with our little girl's feet, making her giggle. It's good to hear that sound coming from her. Every time I've seen my child, she's been so sombre, so quiet. It's almost as if she knows she's been saved.

"I need to tell Fury," I say, my voice pitched low. I don't want to disturb this moment, but I'm eager as fuck to get the ball rolling on this. I want my kid fixed.

"I want to come with you," she tells me, and I can see it takes a whole lot of strength for her to say it.

Is Sasha ready to face her own demons?

She's going to have to stare her past in the face at some

point, the clubhouse is home, but I didn't expect she'd want to do it so soon. My brave girl.

"Okay, baby," I say, my hands moving to her shoulders. Since I got her back, I want to touch her every opportunity I can, to remind myself she's real and that she's here. That Sasha lets me tells me more than her words could. Despite being scared, she's letting me in.

I watch her nibble at her bottom lip as she peers down at Lily-May. "I'll see if Lucy can stay while we're gone."

"There will be a prospect or brother here, too."

Sasha nods and slips out of my touch as her phone finds its way into her hand. I watch as she walks out of the room, leaving me alone with my daughter for the first time.

Lily-May peers up at me as she sucks on her fingers. My kid is so fucking cute. How did me and Sash make something so perfect? I reach my hand out and touch her belly, like I've seen Sasha do before, avoiding the wires. Lily stares up at me with big blue eyes. She doesn't flinch or move away. There's no fear in her eyes, something I'm used to seeing from others, just acceptance. She doesn't see the monster I am and that's liberating in a way I never expected. I doubt she understands who I am to her, but she will in time. Lily-May will never know another day without a father in her life.

The door snicks open behind me, and I don't move my hand, but I do turn my head as Sasha steps back into the room.

"Lucy's on her way."

I return my attention to Lily-May. "You did good with her, Sash. She's so fucking perfect."

It hits me in the gut when she says, "It didn't feel like I was doing good at the time." Sasha moves next to me and I feel her heat at my side. "Especially when she got sick."

I'm not good with words, so I reach out and pull her into

me, engulfing her in my hold. My lips press into her hair. "It ain't your fault she got sick."

"It felt like a punishment."

"For what?"

She peers up at me, tears staining her cheeks. I want to wipe them away, but I don't want to release my hold on her.

"For the recklessness of my life before her. I did a lot of stupid shit I'm not proud of."

"Your lifestyle didn't give Lily-May cancer. It's just one of those things. A shitty hand of cards."

Her thin smile tells me she doesn't believe my words. How the fuck do I convince her she didn't give our daughter this terrible disease?

Lily-May fists her hands against her eyes, rubbing them. I wonder what she would be like without the cancer ravaging her little body. Would she be running around the clubhouse, going from brother to brother, keeping me on my toes? It's hard to gauge whose personality she has inherited, because most of the time she's sleeping or out of it because of the medications. When this is over, I can't wait to get to know my daughter.

Neither of us speaks for a while, just content to watch as Lily-May's eyes flutter shut, so when the door opens behind us, instinctively, I put myself between Sasha, my daughter and the threat. Nothing will touch them ever again.

I relax a little when I see it's Kyle.

"What?" I bark out, annoyed at having our moment ruined and at the fact the fucker didn't knock before barging in.

Kyle doesn't even flinch. Yeah, this one will make a good brother once he's through his probation period.

"That chick with the blonde hair is here."

"It's Lucy," Sasha tells me, her hand coming to my arm, a

silent warning to calm my temper. I must be telegraphing my rage.

I force myself to relax, because neither her nor Lily-May deserve to be subjected to my temper—not today, not after receiving the best news we could ever have hoped for.

Even so, I give Kyle a sharp inclination of my head, telling him without words that it's okay to let her through and one I hope tells him silently I'm pissed off.

Lucy steps into the room, her eyes wild as she takes us both in. As always, she's wearing her hair in a messy topknot, and she has on a sweater that is a size too big and hangs off her, exposing one shoulder.

"I came as soon as you called. What's going on?"

Sasha's mouth splits into a grin and I vow to make her do that every day. She looks so beautiful when she smiles.

"They found a match."

Lucy shrieks, then covers her mouth with both hands. My anger flares as I peer at the cot bed, but Lily-May is out of it still. Luckily.

"Oh my God, I can't believe it." Her voice comes out in a whisper.

"We want to tell him in person that he matched, so can you stay with Lily-May while we do?"

Her head bobs up and down. "Absolutely. I can't believe we have a match."

"Me neither," Sasha says with a smile on her lips, and I can see the relief in her eyes. I feel it too. Since I learnt Fury was a match, the weight on my shoulders seems to have lifted off them. I feel lighter, like for the first time since I learnt Lily-May is sick, I can breathe easily.

I pick up Sasha's leather jacket where it's draped over the back of the chair and hand it to her. She shrugs into it, fixing the collar as she settles it into place.

"We won't be long," she says, unable to tear her eyes from Lily-May.

I feel her reluctance to leave, as does Lucy, because she says, "I'll take good care of her, Sash."

"I know."

I hold my hand out to Sasha and she takes it. There's still a hint of hesitation there, but not enough for me to address it. I know trust will take time to rebuild. My woman was hurt, both physically and emotionally. She has to learn I'm someone she can rely on again. I'll spend a lifetime proving that if I have to.

Because I'm never letting her go again.

Her hand feels so warm and good in mine. She completes me with her touch. I ignore the looks we get as we walk through the hospital. People stare at my kutte, seeing the monster I am. I'm used to being studied like a slide under a microscope, but with Sasha at my side, I want to protect her from this shit. She doesn't seem bothered, though. She walks tall and proud, and why wouldn't she? Her entire life has been embroiled with this MC. Her father was a member; she grew up in this world. She may have been out of it for a few years, but I can see she's going to slot back into it without missing a beat.

When we get outside, I lead her over to the motorcycle parking area. There are a few crotch rockets parked, and two Harleys—mine and Kyle's. I notice the other riders have been careful to park away from us.

I see the flicker of excitement dancing in her eyes as she takes my bike in.

"We're riding?"

"Unless you want to walk."

She shakes her head, then grabs my arm, stopping me. "Are you sure about this?"

I know why she's asking. Having a woman on the back of

my bike is a big deal. It says she's mine. I thought Sasha understood that's where I stood with her. I thought she knew I'd claimed her. I haven't exactly been quiet about the subject.

"I'm sure," I tell her, leaving no room for interpretation.

Her breath seems to catch in her throat and I watch as her eyes dart between me and the Harley.

I've upgraded since she was last on the back of my motorcycle. This model is newer, better and I can see the appreciation she has for it as she runs a hand over the fuel tank.

"This is beautiful, Ty."

"Levi did the body work."

"He did a great job."

I unhook my helmet off the lock on the back and hand it to her.

She turns it over in her hands before raising her eyes to meet mine. "What about you?" she asks.

"Don't give a fuck about protecting my head, but I do care about protecting yours."

She ducks her chin, a smile playing across her mouth before she pulls the helmet on. It's a little too big for her and wobbles a little but it's better than nothing. I'll get her one that fits right.

I climb on the bike and kick the stand up. Then I glance over my shoulder at her expectantly. Having her on the back of my bike is the right thing to do, but it makes me a little nervous. My dickhead brother is still out there somewhere. We'd be easy targets if he chose to take us out while we're riding. I don't think he'd have the balls, but who knows where his head is at.

So far, he's evaded our every attempt to find him. I have men looking for him from across my business dealings—both legal and illegal. I've even put out an alert to the other Sons' chapters, telling them not to help him in case the crazy fucker shows up at another clubhouse seeking sanctuary.

He'll get no help from my allies, I've made sure of that, but my frustration continues to grow as I wait for him to be found. I need him dealt with so I know my woman and child are safe.

Sasha pauses a second before she moves to the pillion on her side and, using my shoulders, settles herself on the back. After three years riding solo it should feel strange to have someone behind me, but it feels normal, like the old days. When her arms slide around my waist, my dick gives a twitch in my jeans. Feeling her press against my back is doing crazy shit to me and images of her beneath me as I pound into her sweet pussy flash through me.

I rev the bike and her arms tighten around my waist. Then, I hit the gas and we take off.

22

SASHA

RIDING behind Tyler brings back so many memories of a time before my heart was torn open by Sin's betrayal. It reminds me that I was once carefree, that I was happy and that I lived in the moment. I miss those days. I miss when I didn't have to worry about things like bone marrow donors and whether my rapist is out there, looking to harm me and my child.

Even with all that swirling around in my brain, it's easy to ignore for the one thought that is dominating my mind: we found a match.

My daughter will survive this.

It's not a guarantee, but it is a chance, and that's all she needs—a chance. If she takes to the transplant, her survival increases more and more with each day. I just can't believe Fury matched. Of all the brothers I would not have imagined he would be the most closely aligned with my daughter genetically.

As Ty said, he's one in a million.

I cling to Tyler as he navigates the bike through traffic, the roar of the Harley pipes loud, the vibrations beneath me strong. This is where I was always happiest, sitting behind him, the open road in front of us. The weight in my chest feels like it's been dislodged, allowing my lungs to inflate properly for the first time in months. I feel freer than I've ever felt as I nuzzle against his back.

Part of me is scared to let him in again. Part of me is terrified of getting hurt, but when it comes to Tyler, I can't deny how I feel. Every time I'm with him my heart feels like it's going to beat out of my chest and my stomach performs somersaults. He makes me feel something good, he makes me feel clean. Sin dirtied me in ways that I can never wash away, but Tyler never makes me feel anything but beautiful and whole. When he looks at me, he sees past the broken, damaged woman to the core of who I am. He sees the old me. I may no longer be that Sasha, but part of her still exists in me, buried deep beneath the filth. Every moment I spend with him, I feel my resolve to keep away weakening, and when he kissed me, I knew it was over. I can't resist this man anymore. I want him. Hell, I need him. So does Lily-May. She needs her father and I know Ty will protect his daughter with his life.

Sitting on the back of his bike confirms the fact he's claimed us both. He would never have me behind him otherwise. These men are precious about who rides bitch on their bikes, so he's making a statement. It's just another way of him proving to me that he's made me his again and that sends tingles through my belly.

Am I ready to be claimed?

I don't know, but what I do know is I don't want him to walk away after this is done. I want him with me and Lil.

I cling tighter to him, as if I can keep him close with my touch and I feel his muscles bunch beneath my hands. He's not unaffected either by this ride and that has my mouth pulling into a grin.

As we approach the clubhouse, I feel my mood slip. The last time I was here, I wasn't sure who Lily-May's father was and I thought no one would believe Sin attacked me. I'm not sure who knows my secret beyond Tyler and Nox, but I don't want to see pity in the eyes of people who were—who are— my family.

When Zack steps out of the security booth and pulls the gate open, my veins turn to ice. Can I do this? Can I walk back into the clubhouse after all this time?

My emotions are mixed.

I have a lot of good memories of this place, as well as the new nightmares that plague me. Sin might not be here, but his presence is embedded in the bricks and mortar of the building. I try to push that aside and remember at one point this was home. It will be again.

Tyler leads the bike over to a space near the side door and puts his feet on the ground. I climb off, my legs a little shaky. It's been so long since I last rode, I feel jellied. He kicks the stand down and pulls the bandanna off his face as I tug his helmet off and hand it back to him.

His eyes rove hungrily over my face as he takes it from me without a word. Without warning, he pulls me into his arms and captures my mouth. I can't stop my body from reacting, from wanting him. Loving Tyler was never an issue. I've always loved him, but knowing I can have him again has my stomach flipping like I'm a love-struck teenager.

It doesn't mean I'm not terrified, because I am. The thought of letting him in again, of getting hurt again scares me to death, but with each passing day, my trust of Tyler is growing more and more.

When he pulls back from my mouth, he's breathless. So am I. His kisses add to the wobbliness in my legs and I cling to his forearms to keep steady as I peer up into his eyes.

"I've missed this," he says quietly.

I can't help but smile. "Me too."

He places the helmet on the back of the bike, then slips his hand into mine, giving me a squeeze before we start walking towards the door. I squint as we move from outside to inside, the change in lighting taking a moment to adjust to.

I steel myself, taking a deep breath as I glance around. I don't know what I expect, but the common room hasn't changed in three years. It's still the same old ratty sofas, the same beat up pool table, the same dirty looking bar and linoleum flooring. The stench of weed is heavy in the air, as is the smell of stale beer and cigarettes. Nostalgia washes through me as I remember all the times I was here as a girl while my father saw to club business, and I feel my spine snapping straight as I step into the shoes of the old Sasha, the woman I was before Sin's attack—the brave, brazen, sassy, don't fuck with me bitch who was devoted to her man and the club. It's hard not to become her again when I'm surrounded by my past. I remember sitting at the table near the door when I got my property patch off Tyler, I remember my first kiss with him in the corner near the pool table, and I remember the first time he told me he loved me by the bar.

There are other memories too. Especially of Priest. My father used to sit at the end of the bar every day. It was always his spot and his face floats across my mind as I stare at the empty seat. How much everything has changed.

When he was alive, he had Daimon's position of Treasurer while Ty's father was President until his death. They were both taken out when a rival club opened fire on them at a bike rally. The Sons burnt that club to the ground in the years after, Tyler leading from the president seat, which he took shortly after his father was gunned down. Ty rebuilt the ranks and restored peace to the club.

I hate that my memory of my father is hazy, and grows

hazier with each passing year. One thing I do remember is that he was amazing with numbers and figures in a way I could never be. He's been dead years now, but his memory still lingers. I miss him every day. Had he still been alive, none of this would have happened. He would have been the one to take care of me when Ty was on that run, not Sin.

I push those thoughts aside. Dwelling on the what ifs doesn't do any good.

As I peer around the room, I see most of the brothers are here, as are a few of the club bunnies. I ignore those skanks and focus on the lads.

"Good to see you back where you belong, Sasha," Titch says, raising a pint glass in my direction.

"You sticking around then?" Daimon asks, and I nod, but my attention goes to the corner of the room, where Fury is sitting alone, twisting a blade between his hands.

I don't even think. I cross the room, intending to throw my arms around him and thank him for saving my daughter's life, but fingers on my bicep pull me up short.

I glance back at Tyler who shakes his head at me. "Fury ain't going to appreciate you touching him, Sash."

Right. He doesn't like that.

"I forgot."

He runs his fingers over his beard and grabs my hand. "Come on."

We head over to Fury's table and Ty pulls up two stools. I take one, he takes the other.

Fury peers up at us. His knife, which he had been sticking in the tabletop, pauses, and I see the confusion in his face.

"Prez?"

Tyler leans forward, clasping his hands together on the tabletop.

"The doc gave us the results of the test. You matched."

Fury's brows draw together. "I matched?"

"Yeah, brother."

He mulls this over for a moment before he says, "Good."

"You going to be okay with the procedures?" Tyler asks. "There's going to be needles."

He stares at the knife in his hand, then his eyes rise to meet mine. "For that little girl, yeah."

I blink back my tears. He's never even met her, but because she's mine, he's embraced her as family.

"I can't thank you enough, Fury."

He grunts, then glances at Tyler. "When?"

"As soon as they have an available spot for you to do the blood test. Whizz might be able to take them instead."

That would probably be safer for everyone involved. Fury might want to help, but his fear of needles isn't going to go away.

"What you're doing will save Lily-May's life," I say, swiping at my eyes. "Thank you."

I watch as Fury twists the knife in his hands, his brow drawing down. "I've never saved someone before."

That thought makes a shiver crawl up my spine. I know these men are not saints. I've been around the club for long enough to know that. I know they sometimes do terrible things, that they are all swimming in the blood of people they've hurt and killed over the years, but I don't care. Fury is family and in this life that counts for something. Family always comes first, which makes what Sin did to me worse. He not only shit on Priest's memory by touching his daughter, but he shit all over his brother by betraying his trust in the worst possible way.

Fury might be cracked, but he's still family, and that means something.

I don't care if he slaughtered ten people, hell a thousand people. He's going to save my daughter's life. His past means nothing to me.

23

RAVAGE

I LEAVE Sasha in the common room to attend church, our club meeting. No one but patched brothers and prospects—if they're invited—attend, and what is talked about never leaves the four walls. It's where we conduct our business and decide on the direction the club is heading in. Today, there's only one topic on the agenda—my shithead brother.

"Tell me someone has good fucking news," I growl out from my place at the head of the table. As my new VP, Nox sits at my right-hand side, Fury, my sergeant-at-arms to my left.

"Little fucker is slippery," Nox says.

"I did get a bead on him moving into Devils territory," Daimon adds from further down the table. "I asked Maverick to keep an eye out, but so far no one's seen shit."

The Devil's Dogs are another London-based club we have a tenuous alliance with. I don't think the Devils would hide my brother and risk pissing us off, not after recovering from their own spat with the Northampton Reapers not that long ago.

I bang my fist on the table and lean across it. "I want that cunt found," I hiss.

"Do you want to tell us why you're so hell-bent on finding him?" Titch asks with a hint of steel in his voice.

I know the lads are getting restless, that they can feel something brewing. I know it because I can feel it too. A storm is coming, and I don't know when, but I know it's going to destroy everything it touches when it lands. Finding my brother before it starts is the key to keeping bloodshed to a minimum.

"It ain't my story to tell, but just know he did something he can't come back from. I want his fucking colours and I want his life."

"Does this have anything to do with Sash being back in town?" Daimon presses, flicking his ash into the ashtray on the tabletop before taking a long drag of his cigarette.

When he gives me his eyes, I see the hardness there—not for me, but for the thought something might have happened to Sasha. Their loyalty to her is a relief to see, especially after I spent the past few years talking her down.

"Just fucking find Sin, yeah?" I snap out. "Let me worry about Sash." I drag my fingers through my hair, which is loose of the tie. "He shouldn't be this fucking hard to pin down."

"The bloke is resourceful," Levi says, "I'll give him that."

Too resourceful. How is he managing to evade us when we have everyone looking? I can't stop the rage from roaring through me. I shove my feet and kick the chair back out of the way before slamming a hand on the table so hard the pain reverberates up my arm.

"Widen the search. Put out a reward for information on him," I yell. "I want him fucking found!"

"We'll find him," Nox says, his voice low, trying to calm my anger. It doesn't work. I'm too fired up.

"He's a fucking risk to Sasha and my daughter! So, you find him and you fucking find him fast. I don't care if we have to tear London apart to get him. Anyone hiding him is fucking dead. Anyone helping him is fucking dead. Do you hear me?"

"Yeah, Rav, I hear you."

I kick over a trash can, sending rubbish spewing into the air, and drag the doors open, my heart galloping in my chest as acid burns through my veins.

"Meeting a-fucking-journed." I throw the words over my shoulder as I storm off in the direction of the common room.

My frustration is rolling through me like hot magma. I can barely control my fury. The longer my brother is out there, the longer this shit drags out for. I want it done. I don't want his murder hanging over my head for weeks. I don't want him out there, risking my child and woman's safety. We're a powerful club. Finding one man shouldn't be this hard a fucking task.

As I shove into the common room, I find Sasha sitting in a booth talking with Briella, Levi's little sister. Levi only patched in after Sash was gone, so Sash and Briella can't know each other, but they're deep in conversation, as if they've been best friends for fucking life.

Sash's eyes raise to me as I stand in the doorway, huffing like a bull. She murmurs something to Brie then slips out of the booth, coming to me. There's no fear in her, despite the fact I'm radiating homicidal levels of rage right now. Her hand comes to my arm and I feel the anger start to leech out of me at her touch. She always did have the power to ground me again.

"What's happened?"

I tear a hand through my hair, which is loose rather than in its usual tie.

"You getting to know Brie?" I avoid the question. I don't want to tell her I'm failing on my promise to keep her safe.

"Ty…" There's warning in her voice as she says my name.

I scrub a hand over my face, knowing I need to give her the truth here, as much as I don't want to. My nerves feel more settled in her presence, as always.

"There's nothing to worry about."

She glares at me, her arms folding over her chest. Her expression tells me she doesn't believe a word coming out of my mouth.

"Don't keep things from me. I can't deal with any more half-truths or lies."

I don't want to dirty her with my words, but there's nothing else I can do. I want her trust. I need it if we're going to move forward.

I blow out a breath and say, "We still can't find Sin, but we're looking every second of every day." I take her hands in mine as I watch her spine stiffen and see the ripple of fear roll through her. "He won't touch you or Lily-May, baby. I promise." My words are hard, emphatic.

It's a promise I fully intend to keep.

I'll destroy my brother before I let him touch a single hair on her or Lily's heads.

I lean down and kiss her. She allows it, and I feel her soften in my arms. I love when she does that. I love the trust she places in me to keep her heart safe and protected. Sasha talks sass and puts this hardened front in place, but beneath it she's got a marshmallow centre. She's easily hurt by the people she cares about. Always was.

When I pull my mouth from hers, I move back enough to trace her face with my eyes.

"While you're here, why don't you take a shower, maybe grab some food?" I tuck a piece of hair behind her ear.

"I want to get back to the hospital."

"I know, but you need to take care of yourself too. You're running on fumes."

I think she's going to argue with me, but after a moment she nods her head.

"Okay."

I kiss her head before taking her hand and leading her through the clubhouse and up the stairs at the back of the building. I have a suite of rooms on the first floor. When Sash and I were together, I bought a house, but after she left, I didn't see the point of keeping it, so I sold it on. I live in the rooms here.

I use the key to open the door and step inside, holding it open for her to follow me. Her eyes are everywhere as she takes in my large king-size bed, the small living area with large screen television and the door off to the en suite bathroom. It's large, roomy—home.

"You decorated," she says, glancing around the space.

I did. When I moved in full time, I had the lads paint it a dark metallic grey on one wall, the rest is cream. I move to pick up some clothes from the floor, tossing them into the hamper at the side of the bed. Not that I've ever done laundry in my life. The club bunnies collect it once a week and return it the next day.

Her eyes move to the hole in the wall I made when I first learnt about Sin's betrayal and her brow arches.

I shrug, then say, "Shower's through there. There should be clean towels on the rack."

She doesn't move, her eyes still roaming around the space.

"What?" I ask her.

"I'm just remembering the last time I was in this room." Her voice sounds a little breathy, and I dredge back through my memory banks. "Do you remember?" she asks, her gaze finding mine.

"We snuck upstairs for a quick fuck before I had to leave on a run." A run that my brother didn't come on. I left him behind to protect my girl. Some protection he was. "Was it… here… it happened?"

I swallow the bile climbing up my throat, heat licking up my skin. Have I slept for three years in the same room she was brutalised in?

The thought makes me sick.

Her demeanour changes instantly. Her arms wrap around her waist and she takes a step from me. I don't like that she's putting distance between us, so I move with her, closing that gap, and take her hand in mine. She doesn't pull away, which I see as a good sign.

"No. It was at the house." Sasha ducks her head, and I hate seeing my strong girl deflating before my eyes. "After you left for the run, Sin took me back there." Her throat works as she speaks and I feel the rage returning, burning through me like fire. I don't want to know the details. Imagining is bad enough. Having the cold hard facts will destroy me.

"I sold it."

Her brow cocks and I see the disbelief in her eyes. "You did?"

"About six months after you left. It didn't feel like home anymore."

I watch Sasha's eyes close as she takes this in. "I'm sorry I left how I did."

My hands come to her face, cupping her cheeks. "You've got fuck all to be sorry about. If I'd known—"

I break off, my temper flaring. I grit my teeth to stop from losing my shit.

"It's in the past, Tyler." Sasha surprises the fuck out of me by rolling to her toes and pressing her mouth to mine.

My fingers move to tangle in her hair, keeping her mouth locked in place. I tug her head back, deepening the angle and devouring her as I do, tasting every inch of her. As I lick along the seam of her mouth, she opens to me, granting me the access I desperately crave. I don't waste any time. I suck her tongue into my mouth and caress along its length as I do. Her movements are a little hesitant at first, but it's like muscle memory kicks in and her arms drape around my neck, pulling me closer.

I want to be inside her now, but I'm aware of the damage my brother might have done to her by taking what wasn't freely given. For that reason, I need to go slow with her, be gentle.

My eyes search hers and I see no reluctance there, so I hoist her into my arms. Sasha's ankles lock around my hips, not breaking contact with her lips.

My cock is hard as a rock in my jeans and I'm desperate to be inside her, desperate to claim fully what's mine, but my movements are hesitant.

She pulls back from my mouth and peers into my face. "I won't break," she whispers.

I study her face, trying to get a read on her thoughts. "You're sure about this?"

"Yes."

"You want to stop, just say the word."

Her smile has my dick twitching, and when her mouth crashes back onto mine, I nearly lose my balance.

I move so we're against the wall, her back to the plaster and she slides down out of my arms. I miss her touch instantly, but she doesn't stay gone long. Her hands fumble on my belly and my muscles ripple as she tugs the hem of my tee free from my jeans. Then her fingers move under the material, ghosting along the bare flesh.

I don't waste time either, sliding my hand up her side to her ribs until I'm circling her breast. My hand curls around it, squeezing. It's not enough, though. I need to feel her skin against mine. I push the material up and her arms follow, so I can pull it over her head. It gets tossed on the floor somewhere behind us. My kutte and shirt follow a second later.

Still kissing her, we move over to the bed and I take her down onto the mattress, climbing on top of her. She feels so good beneath me—soft, warm, willing.

Tugging her bra down to reveal dark nipples, I dip my head and suck one of the little nubs into my mouth, my tongue circling it. Her back arches. My fingers clasp her wrists and I tug them over her head, pinning them against the bed.

Sasha stiffens, her whole body jolting at my touch.

I release my hold instantly and pull back, searching her face. Her eyes are closed and I can see the pain in every line of her face, as if she's reliving a nightmare. Her chest rises and falls in quick succession, her breath ripping out of her.

I lift off her slightly, my heart pounding.

Shit.

"Sash?"

Sasha doesn't open her eyes. I'm not sure if touching her is a good idea, but my hands cup her cheeks.

"Sash, look at me." Her eyes flutter and her glassy gaze focuses on my face. "I'm here. You're safe."

She blinks, seeming to come back into awareness.

"I'm sorry." The rawness of her voice shreds me.

"Don't fucking apologise."

I lift off her and sag onto the bed next to her, my heart muscles still having a workout. Then I pull her into my arms, squeezing her to my chest. Her arms wind around my body and I feel her shaking.

"He's going to pay for every hurt he put on you," I promise her. "Every tear he's made you shed, every pain he's made you feel. I'm going to gut him and make him suffer. I promise you that."

Sasha snuggles against me, and I feel her tears against my bare chest. It guts me, tears my heart from my chest to know my brother caused this.

"Yeah, you'll kill him, Tyler, but at what cost?"

"I don't care about that." And I don't. Will it stain my soul? Yes. But it's a mark I can live with.

"I care about the cost to you." She stumbles over the words as she blurts out, "I love you."

I feel her tension as she says those words. Is she wondering how they'll be taken? I peer down at her, brushing her hair from her face.

"You love me?"

Sasha gives me a half smile. "I never stopped." She traces circles on my chest. "You don't have to say it back."

I take her head in my hands and bring her lips to mine. When I'm done, I rest my forehead against hers and take a deep breath.

Then, I give her the words I've needed to say from the moment she walked back into my life. "I never stopped either, baby."

24

SASHA

TYLER HOLDS me close for so long, just stroking my hair as I lie pressed against his chest. It's been three years, for fuck's sake, but the moment he held my wrists down memories invaded me. It was as if I was there again, reliving my nightmare. It was Sin's hands holding me down as I begged him to stop. It didn't matter how much I pleaded, how much I fought to get free, how much I screamed at him not to do it, he took what he wanted without remorse. Afterwards, all I can remember feeling was numb as he kissed me, as if he were my lover, rather than my rapist. I spent the past three years avoiding touches, building myself back up, but the darkness is creeping back in now, shredding what's left of my control.

In Tyler's arms, I can pretend none of that happened, that my demons are not rising and ready to escape. I can act as if my past is just that—my past—but I can't stop the tears. I feel as if I've got permission to let it all go, to finally break the chains around my soul. They come freely, dripping off the edge of my face onto his bare chest. He doesn't say a word about them, just keeps stroking me.

It feels good, right, being back in his arms again. This is the place I always fitted. This is the place that always felt like home to me.

God, I missed it all so much.

Sin took my world from me. He took my body, my mind, my family and the love of my life. Functioning without Tyler all this time has not been easy. Every night, I thought of him, about what he was up to with the brothers, if they were all okay. Lily-May filled the gap in my heart, but there was always something else missing—Tyler. I loved him from the moment I was old enough to understand what love was. That never disappeared, even when he was spitting venom at me and calling me a whore. I knew that was the anger speaking. I did what only a few people have ever managed to do—I hurt him. Walking away broke both of us.

I have to accept some of the blame. I should have had more faith in the man, in *us*. I should have believed that if he knew the truth, he would have protected me, not thrown me away like Sin said he would. Out of everything, that was the worst thing Sin did to me. He made me doubt my reality. He made me lose faith in my family and in the man I loved.

Since he found out my secret, he's been the old Tyler with me. Each touch, each look reminds me of how it was between us, and it's making me realise how much I miss what we had.

"You okay?" he asks, pressing his mouth to my hair.

I nod. "Thank you."

"For what?"

"Understanding."

His body tenses a little under me and he huffs out a breath. "Fucking Sin."

I lift slightly off him, so I can glance up the lines of his chest to his face.

"Forget about him. All I care about is you and Lily."

"I ain't forgetting what he did to you. I ain't ever forgetting that shit."

His words are like a knife to the belly. I disentangle myself from his hold and push to the edge of the mattress, raking my fingers through my hair.

"What?" he demands, his tone sharp.

"You can't forget it," I tell him, my voice filled with sadness. "We can never have a relationship if every time you look at me you see me as a victim. It'll tear you apart."

It'll tear *us* apart.

I feel the bed dip behind me and then his hands are sweeping my hair back from my neck.

"I don't look at you and see a victim. I see a strong as fuck woman who survived hell and still managed to bring our beautiful fucking daughter up to be just as strong."

Tears well in my eyes at his words. "Ty…"

"Sin'll die for what he did, not because he made you a victim, darlin', but because he took something he didn't have the right to take." He kisses my neck and I tilt my head to give him better access. His lips trail up the column of my throat, sending shivers through me. Just as I'm getting into it, he pulls back.

"Go and shower," he says in a soft voice I barely recognise. "Then we'll go back up to the hospital to be with Lily-May."

"I'm not broken," I tell him, needing him to know that, needing him to see me as strong. I can't stand being with him if he thinks I'm this damaged little girl.

"I know."

"I mean it, Tyler. I'm not broken," I repeat, my words snarling out of me. I don't want to be seen as weak. I don't want what happened to me to be the first thing people see when they look at me. "I survived what he did to me, and I came out the other side a different person, but I'm tougher now."

I don't know if I'm saying the words to convince him or me, but speaking them helps ease some of the tightness in my chest.

"I see that."

I push off the bed and snag my tee off the floor. "Do you?"

He moves too, his hands coming to land on my shoulders, stopping my frantic movements. "I don't see what he did to you. I see you, being strong, getting your shit together for our daughter. You should never have had to go through that alone. I'm sorry you did, because I should have been there with you. I *would* have been there with you."

I close my eyes for a brief moment, pain lancing through my chest, before I peer up at him. "I should have let you, but after... fuck, I was a mess. I couldn't deal with anything. Sin made me believe you'd never listen to me, that you wouldn't believe a word I said. I shouldn't have let him get in my head like that."

"I get why you did, but you shouldn't have shut me out, but now that you're back you have to know I ain't going anywhere."

I peer up at him as I scrape my teeth across my bottom lip. "I don't want you to go anywhere."

He closes the space between us, capturing my mouth and I melt against him as his fingers thread into my hair. I want to have him inside me, but that tingle of fear bites just on the edge of my awareness. Losing control again scares me. Keeping it is key.

"Get on the bed," I order him.

"Sash..."

"Get on the bed," I repeat.

"You don't have to do this."

"I don't want him to take anything else from me, especially not this—not us."

He lets out a breath, and then reluctantly climbs onto the bed. I move slowly towards him, my heart pounding. This isn't Sin. It's Tyler, and I know he won't hurt me.

I push that bastard out of my head and focus on the beautiful man lying on the bed, his jeans low on his hips, his inked-up chest staring back at me. I move to his belt and slowly undo it. He watches me with heated eyes and lifts his hips as I tug the denim down his legs. I remove his motorcycle boots, tossing them to the carpet, then I pull his jeans the rest of the way down, pooling them on the floor next to his boots.

His hands interlace behind his head as he watches me crawl back up his body to his boxers. I meet his gaze. He's watching me like a cornered animal, as if he expects me to lose my shit. I hate that he is, but we're both going to have to find our way through this mess. I take a steadying breath, before I pull the material down his legs again and off the end of his feet. His cock springs free, the length hard, long, veiny and beautiful. I wrap my mouth around the shaft, my hand holding the root as I swipe my tongue over the slit. He jerks his hips, his breath ripping out of him. I grin and move my tongue again over his end, tasting the salty precum that's starting to leak from the head.

Tyler moves my hair aside, fisting its short length in one hand as I hollow my cheeks out and take his cock further down my throat. He growls a curse.

"Babe, you keep this up, I'm going to come in your mouth."

Ignoring his words, I swipe my tongue over the head of his shaft, feeling triumphant when his hips twitch again. I suck harder, moving my hand at the base of his dick in a slight twist that has him cursing under his breath.

I mix it up between twisting, licking and fondling his balls until he's writhing beneath me. Then his hips flex once more and he shoots his load into my mouth. I take it all, everything he has to give, swallowing it down, the saltiness coating my tongue. When he stills, I peer up the length of his body and see his arm is draped over his eyes and his chest is heaving.

"Fuck," he mutters.

I smile when he drops his arm and looks at me through glazed eyes.

"That was… I forgot how good it could be between us." He starts to move, grabbing my hips to pull me closer, but I shake my head.

"Ty…"

I'm not ready for more yet, but I will be, in time.

He leans forward and pulls me to him, then he kisses my forehead.

"We've got forever, sweetheart."

And this is why I love this man, because he gets it. He gets me, and you can't buy that kind of understanding. Tyler says I'm his, but that works both ways. He's mine and I'm not letting go of him either.

25

RAVAGE

"I SHOULD GET in the shower. I don't want to leave Lily-May too long."

Sasha's warm breath tickles my chest, making my muscles quiver. I don't want to move yet. My mind is still blown from the feel of her lips around my cock, but I understand her worry about leaving our daughter alone. I don't like the thought either, especially with Sin still out there.

I brush the hair from her face, the soft strands trailing through my fingers, as my gaze roams over her features. How did I last three years without her? She's beautiful and she's mine. I should never have forgotten that. I want to kick my own arse, drag her father back from the grave to hand me the punishment I deserve for turning my back on his daughter. After she left, I should have looked for her. I should never have given her up so easily.

Darkness claws at my heart when I realise what my pride nearly cost me. I have a daughter. I may never have found out if she wasn't sick and that thought tears at my heart. It also pisses me off. I may never have found out who and what my brother really is either. The dagger he has lodged in my back has been twisted deeper over the years. How many other women has he gone too far with? Is Sasha his only victim? Are there others he's abused? The thought makes bile rise in my throat. We aren't good men. The darkness claimed us a long time ago, but it's a rule cast in iron that we don't hurt women.

My thoughts scatter as Sasha dips her head and takes my mouth. It's a soft, wet kiss that has my dick twitching. Then again, everything about this woman makes me hard. The urge to claim her fully is a battle, but I can't. Not yet. She's not ready, but she will be soon.

I hope eventually my touches will erase his, that I'll consume her until she can only see me. I hope that she'll know she belongs to me and only me.

The rapping of knuckles on the door has both our heads twisting towards it.

"Go and shower, sweetheart."

Sasha leans in to kiss me once more before she pushes up off the bed, her eyes straying towards the door. I watch her long legs as she walks into the bathroom, waiting until I hear the door snick shut before I make my body start to move. Snagging my boxers off the floor, I pull them on quickly over my semi hard-on, before stepping into my jeans, buttoning them as I walk to the door.

When I pull it open, I'm greeted by Nox leaning both forearms against the top of the door frame.

He eyes me, his gaze taking in my rumpled hair, my bare chest and then going beyond me to the bed.

He brings his attention back to me and I don't miss the slight curl of his lip. "Don't fucking hurt her."

His tone grates on my nerves. What the fuck does it have to do with him what me and Sasha do?

"Ain't your business, Nox." My voice is pitched low, caution crackling through the words.

He doesn't take the warning.

"Sash is one of us. That makes it my business."

I narrow my gaze at him, my mouth pulling into a tight line as my nostrils flare.

"Don't ever fucking question me."

We both stare at each other. After a few moments, Nox nods tersely before he scrubs a hand over his jaw. I see the tension radiating in every line of his body. "We've got a lead on Sin."

My stomach lurches and icy talons dig into my heart at his words.

"You didn't think to fucking start with that?"

I quickly move back into the room and snag a clean tee from the dresser. It goes over my head before I grab my kutte from where I dropped it earlier. I shrug into it. The old leather, soft from years of wear, fits my body like a glove. The smell of cigarettes, marijuana and stale beer clings to the material. It's a reassuring smell that reminds me of who I am. Of what I am.

I drag open the top drawer of my dresser and grab my knife. Bending at the waist, I slide the sheath into my boot, pulling the leg of my jeans over the top of it.

When I straighten, I push past Nox. "Let's fucking go."

I know he's behind me as I walk out of the clubhouse, my mind on what I'm going to have to do. Killing my brother has to happen. I've never given a single thought for any life I've taken, but I know this one will add to the demons that plague me. I raised that boy like he was my own, so taking his life isn't something I do lightly, but he signed his own death when he raped Sasha and took her from me, from her family, from her life. He destroyed everything about her with that one act and now I will destroy him. I'll end his life as payment and not just for Sasha, but for her father too. If Priest was still around, he would have hung Sin up and gutted him, made him pay for days.

As we approach our bikes, I see my other brothers are mounted and ready to ride. Daimon gives me a look as I climb on my Harley, no doubt wondering how level I am. Titch, Levi and Whizz are pulling their helmets on while Fury sits astride his bike, ready, waiting. My sergeant-at-arms won't have to get his hands dirty today. No, Sin is all mine.

I look at each of their faces. This is what it's all about—having brothers at my back. This right here is what makes us the club we are, what makes us the Untamed Sons.

I tie my skull bandanna around my neck and tug it up over my face. Swinging my leg over the bike, I sit gripping the handles until my knuckles turn white as I wait for Nox to get seated on his. As we start up our engines, the roar of Harley pipes is loud, the smell of the engine oil heavy in the air. It drowns out everything else, clearing my head, helping me to focus on the task ahead.

Nox rolls out of the compound first, followed by me then Fury and Daimon. Titch, Whizz and Levi take the rear, watching our arses.

London is busy, cars and buses choking the roads. The smog lingers in the air, and would catch the back of my throat if it wasn't for the material covering my face.

We weave through the vehicles as exhausts splutter fumes into the air. I don't like lane splitting when we're riding as a group, but I want to get to my brother fast, which means I don't want to be sitting in gridlock.

I follow Nox closely, in sync with his movements as he navigates through the line of vehicles. I can hear the bikes behind me, a reassuring presence at my back as Nox leads us. It feels strange to ride behind him. My place is usually up front, leading, but I don't know where the fuck we're going.

My thoughts should be racing, but I feel oddly calm as we head towards the place where my brother was last seen. I have no idea how things will go down, but what I do know is I can taste vengeance on my tongue. It burns like hot ash.

I'm coming for you, brother.

Eventually, Nox pulls the bike into the parking area of an abandoned warehouse and rolls to a stop. I move in next to him and tug the bandanna down as I peer up at the crumbling brickwork and smashed windowpanes. It doesn't look like anyone has been using the place for a while. The weeds are thick on the ground and graffiti is spray-painted on the exterior wall. There's a heavy-set door on the front that looks secure, but from here I can see it's been unscrewed from the hinges and is leaning against the frame. In this life, I learnt a long time ago not to underestimate anything. It might look safe, abandoned, but that doesn't mean shit.

I kick down the stand and cut my engine, the others doing the same. My eyes lock on the building and my lip curls into a snarl. Before Sasha came back, the thought of my brother being holed up somewhere like this would have made my blood boil. I did everything for us never to return to a place like this. Now, I can't help thinking this shithole is too good for him.

Tugging my helmet off, I climb off the bike and pull my knife from my boot.

"You know I've got your back, Prez, but if I'm taking another brother's life, pulling his kutte off his back and taking everything that makes him blood to us then I've got to know what I'm doing it for."

I glance at my brothers, seeing the same resolute expressions staring back at me. They're not my brothers by blood, but by a bond that runs deeper—loyalty. Which is why Titch's question doesn't surprise me.

I shift my gaze towards Nox who lifts his shoulders

slightly. Bylaws say a brother can't harm another brother. I should have told them when I first found out, but I didn't want Sasha's life out there for gossip.

It's Nox who speaks, saving me from having to say the words I can't say, saving me from breaking her confidence. His arms fold over his chest, his mouth turning down at the corners, as if he's tasting something rotten. "He raped Sasha."

The finality of how he says it makes my body jolt. I'll never get used to hearing those words, I'll never get used to knowing what he did to her, knowing he took her against her will. Icy claws dig into my heart and tear it apart. It's going to haunt me for the rest of my days, as much as I tell Sasha it won't. I can never forgive or forget what was done to her.

"The fuck?" Titch's voice raises an octave, his expression twisting in disgust. "When?"

Nox lets out a heavy breath and I can see how difficult he's finding this. I don't blame him. My words are stuck in my throat, refusing to come out. "Right before she took off. She didn't betray us or Prez. Sin fucking made her feel like we weren't behind her, that we wouldn't believe her."

"That's why you kicked the shit out of him?" Whizz asks me, his tone sombre.

"I kicked the shit out of him because he fucking lied and told me she came on to him. She was my old lady."

I don't need to say anything else. Everyone brought into this world knows you don't touch a brother's old lady—even if they are fucking begging for it.

"Fuck."

"You don't tell anyone this happened," I growl out, pointing my finger around the brothers. "You don't tell her that you know either."

I don't want this shit staining her further. I don't want them looking at her with pity or remorse, seeing only what my pig brother did and not her. It's what Sasha is most afraid of—being seen as a victim.

Fury's hands are fisted at his side and I can see they're starting to shake.

I brace, in case he decides to explode.

"He raped her?" He breathes out the words on a deadly growl that has my spine snapping straight, my attention ready. Fury's been known to flip his shit without warning before, so I'm prepared in case he does. I wouldn't blame him if he did. That same rage he's feeling right now still burns through my veins.

"Yeah," I confirm.

His mouth twists into an ugly grimace as he asks, "He hurt her?"

"Yeah," I repeat.

He lets out a growl before he draws his arm back and stabs his knife into the door with so much force it quivers when he lets go of the handle.

"Sin has to die," he hisses out, getting in my face. It's rare to see Fury anything but controlled, even his rage is usually controlled, but he always did have a soft spot for my woman. All the guys do. Sash grew up a club brat, always hanging around the clubhouse when she was a kid, trying to get Priest's attention. As Sash got older, she was there with me, trying to get mine. Some of the guys have known her since she was a kid with pigtails in her hair. Others she's known since they took the prospect kutte. Sasha was a huge part of our world... until she wasn't. Her leaving left a hole for us all.

I don't like being crowded, so I push Fury back out of my space and he goes back on a foot, his eyes still blazing fire.

"He has to die," Daimon agrees, his mouth pulled down into a dark grimace. He rakes his fingers through his hair before he taps his fingers against the thigh of his jeans, a clear sign he wants a smoke.

"He's going to," I assure them all. Sin will die, because there's no other option.

I step towards the door and tug Fury's blade free of the wood, handing it back to him, then I take a deep breath and pull it aside.

As soon as I step into the darkened space, I can smell the scent of stagnant water and something murky, like the place has been empty for a while. I let my eyes adjust to the change in lighting for a moment, then allow my gaze to roam around the empty space. The floor is littered with bits of junk and there's a few pieces of old machinery in one corner that look rusted and have been tagged with spray paint.

I don't bother with stealth. Our bikes are not quiet, so if Sin is here, he will have heard us riding in. I hope he's trembling in fear, just like he must have made Sasha when he held her down.

We move as a unit, watching each other's backs as we go, but there's nothing and no one here. I'm giving up hope until we step into a small office room off the main floor. Instantly, I'm hit with a smell that clogs my throat, an acrid stench that makes my stomach revolt. I recognise it immediately.

Something is dead.

There's a dirty mattress on the floor that is stained with a dark brown patch. Blood. On the floor are discarded medicine packages and what looks like bloodied bandages. I kick over a food tray from a pre-packaged meal and glance at the finished bottles of water. He's been here, licking his wounds.

I follow a trail of old blood drops behind a wall and find the half-decomposed body slumped against the plaster. The smell nearly knocks me off my feet.

The back of my hand covers my mouth and nose, trying to protect my senses from the stench as I stare at the body. It's not Sin. Even through the decay I can tell that. There's no ink on what's left of his skin and the clothes are all wrong.

Who it is, I don't know? His dirty clothes are stained with dried dark brown blood and other bodily fluids.

Likely this poor bastard was living here before Sin decided to take up residence. Just another innocent life he's destroyed.

I kick the body, letting my frustration out. It sags to one side, more fluids flowing.

"It ain't him," Daimon says as he steps back from the mess, his nose wrinkling.

"If Sin was here," Levi peers around the space, "he's gone now."

I feel my rage starting to build. "Why the fuck are we always days behind this cunt?"

"He's got to have help." Daimon glances at me. "He can't be ahead of us without someone feeding him information."

"Maybe one of the prospects," Titch says. "Those fuckers would do whatever a patched brother asked."

I shake my head. "I told everyone Sin was not to be helped. If someone is helping him, they're dead."

I walk back into the other part of the room and look for clues, anything that might indicate Sin was here. Something catches my eye. I move over to the edge of the dirty mattress and crouch down. I pull it out and turn it over. It's a couple of rumpled photographs. The first one is at a club cook out, one of many we've had over the years. I remember the photograph being taken, even though it was years ago because it was just after I gave her my property patch.

My face has been scratched out.

There's another photograph of me and Sasha in the common room, although I don't remember this one being taken. My face is again scratched out.

Anger rolls through me like a tidal wave.

How long has this fucker been obsessed with my girl?

If he left these behind, I'm guessing it's because he was in a hurry. Did we only just miss him?

Nox takes the photographs off me and my hands go to the back of my head.

"Fuck!" The word echoes around the empty space, reverberating through the crumbling brickwork. Frustration burns through me as I try to control my pounding heart.

"Rav, this is bad," Nox mutters as he turns the images over in his hands.

"You think I don't know that?"

Whizz peers over Nox's shoulders. "This is some crazy level of obsession, Prez. Sin ain't right in the head."

"Who's with Sasha now?" Titch asks.

"Zack."

"Where the hell did that intel come from saying he was here?" Daimon rakes his fingers through his hair, then taps his fingers on his thighs.

"It was a contact of Zack's…" Nox's mouth pulls into a grimace as panic starts to claw up my throat.

Did we walk right into his trap? Was luring us here just a ploy to get us out of the way, giving him a straight run at Sasha?

"That fucking cunt got us out of the clubhouse," Daimon snarls.

"Where Sasha is alone. Fuck! We need to get back, now," I growl at my brothers and then storm out of the room, bellowing my rage.

SASHA

I COME out of the shower and find Tyler gone. His jeans and kutte are both missing from where they were left on the floor, and his phone is no longer on the bedside table.

I grit my teeth. This is the life I remember. Being left behind without a word, never explaining his actions. "Club business". This is what I signed up for, but it still grates a little. Would it have killed him to say goodbye?

Moving over to his dresser, I pull the top drawer open and find a clean tee and some joggers. I don't miss the assortment of knives in the bottom, but I ignore them. I'm well aware Tyler isn't exactly a Boy Scout.

I pull the joggers on, settling the waistband on my hips, liking the way his clothes feel on me and hoping he won't be pissed I went rummaging through his stuff. They're a little big on me. I have to tie the drawstring to keep them up and the tee hangs off me, but they're fresh. I don't even want to think about how they get laundered. I don't think Ty knows how a washing machine works.

Dressed, I pull my wet hair into a sloppy topknot and head out of the room.

The clubhouse is quiet and I find myself in the common room alone. There's not a single brother in sight.

"Great," I mutter.

I need to get back to the hospital and make sure Lil is all right and since Ty was my ride here, I guess I'm going to have to figure out an alternative.

Just as I'm about to pull my phone out and dial a cab, Zack strolls in. The prospect eyes me as he moves.

"Hey, where'd everyone go?" I ask, peering up from my screen.

"Out."

I roll my eyes. "I figured that much out on my own, thanks." The sarcasm drips from my words. I can't help myself.

"You know, maybe you should watch your mouth."

My brows raise and I return my attention to my phone as I mutter out, "Wow, did you finally find your balls, baby biker?"

"I see you haven't changed at all," a familiar voice says, stepping out from the shadows of the bar. My heart stops dead in my chest and my hands are suddenly damp as I stare at Sin. "Three years on and you're still a fucking bitch."

He looks a mess, his face a mass of yellowing bruises and scabbed over cuts. I don't miss that he holds himself, his hand around his chest as if he's still hurting. Good. I hope Ty broke every bone in his fucking body. It still wouldn't come close to the pain I suffered, to the pain I still suffer.

But coming face to face with my rapist without the buffer of Ty or Nox here has my stomach twisting and my guts rolling. I take a couple of shaky steps back, putting the nearest table between us as my mouth dries out. Fear clamps its hold around my heart so I can barely take a breath in and nausea climbs up my throat.

Fuck. What the hell is he doing here?

I take another step back as he moves towards me, my nightmare continuing to play on a loop. He's not a figment of my imagination. He's really fucking here.

His mouth pulls into a macabre grin.

"No hello?"

Zack glances between the two of us, and I can see it dawning on him that something isn't right here. "Look, man, I only let you in to get your shit and I only did that out of respect for the fact you sponsored me to take the prospect kutte, but you don't talk to her. Rav'll beat us both. Everyone was told not to let you in the building."

"He'll do more than beat you. Kiss your pathetic life goodbye," I snarl out. My heart is pounding so hard now I can barely draw a full breath in without pain lancing through my chest.

"You've got to go, Sin," Zack says, his voice filled with desperation. "You're going to cost me my colours."

The kid is seriously naïve if he thinks that's all he's going to lose. Tyler doesn't do well with betrayal and he'll see this as one.

Sin turns and before I can react, I see the flash of metal and hear the loud pop ricochet off the walls with the unmistakeable sound of a gun being fired.

I jolt as Zack slides to his knees, blood pouring from his forehead before he falls flat on his face. Blood splatters up the wall behind him, along with bits of skull and brain.

Shock roots me to the floor and bile churns in my gut. I grew up in a club that lives on the wrong side of the law. I've seen my share of violence. I've even seen people die, but I didn't expect Sin to kill him like that. The poor kid didn't stand a chance.

"Fuck," I mutter, the word coming out on a shaky gasp.

Sin glances back at me, a grin playing across his face. I don't think. I run, tossing chairs behind me as I go to slow him down. I expect to feel the burn of a bullet in my back, but I don't. I barely reach the door before a hand fists into my hair and drags me back. My scalp burning like a hundred small fires are singeing through my roots.

"Where are you going, Sash?" he hisses in my ear as he drags me close. I hate the way he says my name, I hate the way his breath is warm against my cheek. It makes my stomach swirl. "We ain't done here."

Fear claws up my spine as I'm thrown back into that day. Images of him holding me down as he pushed himself inside me without remorse flood me, and I can hardly breathe.

"Stop!"

No surprise, he doesn't. Ignoring my pleas, he drags me back and I claw at his hands, trying to remove his hold on my hair. He doesn't let go. If anything, his grip becomes more ironclad. Still, I kick and hit out at him. I'm not going down without a fight. I'm not the girl I was three years ago, and that's because of him. I'm stronger, and knowing I have Ty and the club behind me, that I have everything to live for, pushes me to fight.

I don't go easily. I battle hard against Sin, but when he pushes the gun into my side I freeze. If he shot Zack without remorse, I doubt he'd be fazed by putting a bullet in me. Blue eyes flash before my own, her smile, her beautiful curls. I have to live for my daughter.

He pulls me against him and my skin crawls at his touch. Shuddering in his hold, I feel his filth all over me and try to shrink away from his hands, but I can't—not with the kiss of steel against my side.

"You're going to walk out of here willingly or I'm going to shoot you. Then I'll find Rav and shoot him. I might even pay our daughter a visit."

I don't tell him she's not his. Those words falling from his lips make me submit. He will not touch my child or go near her. His filth stays away from her.

I swallow bile. "Okay, okay." My heart flutters in my throat as I stumble over the debris covering the common room floor. I have no idea what his plan is, but I know if I leave the clubhouse I'm fucked.

Sin tugs me and I move on unsteady feet towards the door. My mind is racing, but I can't latch onto a single idea of how to get out of this. I know I have to fight.

As soon as we step outside, I kick my foot back between his legs, hitting him in the dick as hard as I can. I feel a hint of satisfaction as he doubles over with a groan.

Taking off as fast as I can, I sprint towards the compound gates. My legs burn as I pump faster, adrenaline fuelling my movements.

Then a force slams into my back and I go down hard, my knees slamming off the tarmac. Pain ricochets through my bones, jarring me, and I can't stop the cry that escapes my mouth.

I barely have time to think before he's on top of me, straddling my hips. My face is pushed into the ground, scratching up my cheek and I breathe in the smell of the asphalt.

My breath see-saws out of me as I lie there helpless beneath his bulk. No, no, no. I won't let him do this to me again. I won't. His hand goes to the back of my neck and his mouth moves to my ear.

"You're really testing my fucking patience, bitch."

Short-lived relief floods me when he lifts off me and drags me up. I scrape my hands against the ground and pain burns through my palms. As soon as I'm upright, he brings the gun down hard. It slams into my face with enough force to make me see stars. I stumble as my vision darkens and pain throbs through my head. His bruising grip on my arm is all that keeps me on my feet.

Warmth spreads down my face. I swipe at it and my fingers come away covered in red. Blood. I feel dazed, my head dizzy as he pulls me towards the parking area.

I can barely see through the film of red dripping into my eyes as I'm pushed into a vehicle, Sin climbing in after me. He holds the gun on me as he starts the engine.

I'm completely fucked.

RAVAGE

My heart sits in my throat the entire ride back to the clubhouse. Nervous energy tingles through me as my bike rumbles beneath me. I know he's going after her. I can feel it in my soul. I just hope like fuck we're not too late.

I have no clue what to expect as we pull down the road, but I see the main gate is open. Immediately, I go on alert, my stomach churning. The gate is never fucking open.

As the bikes roar past the security booth, I see it's empty. Where the fuck is the kid? Zack's supposed to be here. He's out for this. No second fucking chances.

Fear licks a path up my spine as I stop my bike near the door and kick the stand down. It's not something I usually experience. Like oil and water, it doesn't belong in me. This life has taught me to be unafraid. I don't fear the Grim Reaper. I've been tortured by an enemy club and I still didn't talk, and I've faced the end of a gun barrel on more than one occasion. Fear never raised its ugly head until now.

Praying to the fuckers in the sky I don't believe in that Sasha is still in the shower or crashed on my bed, I don't bother to pull the keys from the engine, but I drag my helmet off as I run towards the door. My boot steps are loud as the rumbling of the Harleys dies down.

My brothers yell at me to stop, warning me to be cautious before entering the building, but I don't listen. The devil himself could be behind that door and he wouldn't stop me. My heart is galloping in my chest, fear that something might have happened to Sasha fuelling my long strides. I shove through the door and when I step inside, my stomach fills with ice.

The room has been turned over, chairs flipped the wrong way up, tables upturned. A chill works its way up from my feet. What the fuck happened?

I hear movement behind me as my brothers pile into the room, but I don't pay them any attention, instead taking in the destruction. A fight happened here.

Sasha?

"Shit, Rav!"

I move around the fallen chairs, tossing the debris aside to move towards Daimon who is kneeling at the side of the bar.

Zack is crumpled on the floor faced down, a pool of sticky blood around his head. The metallic scent of it clings to the back of my throat and I cough, trying to clear it from my sinuses. Whizz crouches down, taking in the mess of brain and blood matted into his hair around a large ugly looking exit wound.

My eyes trail over the blood sprayed up the wall and anger replaces every other emotion as it flares through me, a storm brewing.

Sasha.

Without thinking, I turn and rush towards the common room doors, ignoring Day and Nox yelling after me. My only salvation is the thought that if Sasha is still here maybe she was able to hide. Maybe she's still safe. She grew up in the club, she knew what to do if we were attacked. Maybe she got to safety.

I call her name as I rush up the corridors, my heart dancing in my throat. My voice is pitched higher than usual and I hear the anxiety in my tone. I don't give a fuck. My only focus is on finding my woman.

The further I get from the common room the more my fear tears at me. She's not here. She would have heard me shouting and come to me by now, but my voice just roars off the walls around me only to be met by my echo.

When I push into my room, her smell surrounds me, still lingering in the air, but there's no sign of her. It's like a bullet to the chest as I take in her clothes draped on the end of the bed. At the sight of it my legs nearly give way. He's taken her. Under my watch he came into my clubhouse and took my woman.

"She's not here?" Nox demands as he pushes into the room, Daimon and Fury on his heels.

I close my eyes, asking the universe for patience, but I don't find it. My rage, my frustration, my fear pours out of me. I tug at the dresser, pulling it over. It crashes to the carpet hard enough to vibrate through the floor. It doesn't do anything to help soothe the demons rising in me.

"We need to find her! Now!"

"We don't know it was Sin who did this." Daimon is all about facts and reasons. We have enemies. You don't live this life without them, but everything is screaming at me that this was my brother. I know he took Sasha.

"That cunt has her."

Fear of what Sin might do to her washes through me. My brother hates me. It's clear from the photographs how deep that hate runs. Is this why he raped her? To hurt me? Questions assail my mind and I have no answers to any of them.

All I know is I promised Sasha I'd protect her and now she's in danger.

Failure weighs on my shoulders like I'm carrying a ten-tonne anvil. I can't let her down again. I already fucked up once. I left her with a monster and she got hurt. Now, I've left her in his path again.

"Fuck!" I scream to the empty walls.

Sin started this battle, but now, I'm going to bring the fucking war, and there can only be one winner.

I push out of my room and head back down to the common area. Titch and Whizz are attempting to clean up the mess of Zack's body.

Levi steps towards me. "I found this."

He hands me a mobile phone. I swipe the screen and the background photo pops up. It's Lily-May. Fuck. This is Sash's phone. A glacial cold wraps itself around my throat, squeezing until I can hardly breathe. In my life, I've faced situations that were so bad I thought I wasn't walking out of them. I've been tortured, I've been hurt, but I've never felt fear like this. I don't know who my brother is anymore. I can't predict what he'll do next and that sends a wave of terror through me. What the hell is he doing to my woman? He's already proved he has no trouble taking from her something that isn't given freely. He shot Zack in the fucking head. Now, he's spiralling knowing his life is on a countdown, what will he do to her?

"Zack was helping Sin," I mutter. "See if he's got his phone on him. There might be clues as to where my brother was going."

Whizz digs in Zack's pockets and comes out with a mobile phone. He uses Zack's finger to unlock the finger-print scanner and then starts swiping through the phone.

Nox comes to my side, his hand moving to my shoulder. "We'll find them."

"He could be anywhere."

"You know this kid better than anyone, Rav. Where the fuck would he take her?"

I dip my head, letting my thoughts run. He's right. I know Sin better than he probably knows himself. At least I thought I did. Now, I don't think I knew him at all. The little brother I knew isn't a rapist piece of shit. He was my teammate, my wingman, my fucking blood. It was all an illusion, a mask he wore. Now he's removed it, he's showing me the truth, and it's a truth that is bringing me to my knees piece by piece. There's so much anger towards me, I still don't fucking understand why. I raised him, kept him safe when we had nothing. I went without food so he could eat. The first ten years of my life were a nightmare. Dad was a member of the Sons, but he was mostly absent, off on runs or doing time. We barely saw him. He rarely remembered he had two sons at home. We spent as much time as we could at the clubhouse with Sash and Nox—our friendships cemented by our shared histories of having parents who were absent, busy or didn't give a fuck, but I was finally happy—with Sasha. Didn't he want that for me? Her leaving for the past three years was probably the only thing that kept her safe from his obsession, and that scares the shit out of me.

We didn't have the easiest upbringing, but that doesn't excuse what he's become, what he did to Sasha. The evil control he exerted over her by taking her body against her will can't be excused.

I did the best I could with that kid. I built us a life. I didn't expect him to try to ruin mine by taking the only thing I gave a shit about from me. Growing up, Mum was an addict. We didn't have anything, sometimes not even enough food to eat. I'd take the beatings to protect Sin, to keep him from getting hurt. We'd sleep rough a lot of the time to get out of the house to avoid the steady stream of Johns she had coming through.

One night, Mum battered me so badly, Sin didn't know what the hell to do, so he called Priest, who got Dad. He took one look at me and lost his shit. I don't know what the fuck he said to our bitch of a mother, but after that we lived with him. Things got better, but they still weren't fantastic. Dad didn't know how to parent. He was always knee deep in pussy and booze, but at least he wasn't violent to us. I continued to take care of my brother, trying everything to make his life better. What the fuck did I do that was so bad, that made him betray me in a way that hurts more than a knife to the stomach? I'd rather he'd gutted me alive.

"He'd go back to the warehouse we just left," I say. "He wouldn't think we'd look there again."

"Let's mount up," Nox orders, stepping easily into his VP role. "We'll find them, Rav. I promise."

Yeah, we'll find them, but will it be too late?

SASHA

MY HEAD IS THROBBING, the pain radiating down my cheek and jaw. I can barely see through the blood that's still pouring down my face. I risk sliding my gaze sideways and glance quickly at Sin. He's driving, one hand on the steering wheel, the other on his lap, pointing the gun in my direction —a gun he used to kill Zack. My stomach roils.

I face forward, watching the traffic passing on the other side of the road, dizziness washing over me. I can barely focus on anything other than taking steadying breaths. I'm scared, but if Sin thinks he's going to hurt me without a fight, he's dead wrong. I won't go down without a fight.

I try to come up with a plan, try to remember everything my father and the guys taught me growing up about how to protect myself, but it gets lost in my dazed thoughts.

A glacial hand squeezes my heart as he pulls the car off onto a single track. As we move further from the road and away from civilisation, my fear starts to grow. My shoulders hunch as I realise just how far from the road we are. No one will come down here.

My eyes shift to the large brick building in front of us and

I feel a wave of nausea spread through my body. It's falling apart, the mortar crumbling, the windows put through. There are weeds growing through the cracked concrete and the walls have been tagged by someone called 'Lucky'.

I peer through the windscreen, my heart thrumming beneath my ribs. This is where he's taking me? My plans to escape die and my mouth dries as he stops the engine, pulling the keys from the ignition. They disappear into the inside pocket of his kutte. He doesn't deserve that leather. He was never a brother, a Son. He's a fucking backstabbing bastard.

My mouth pulls into a grimace as I roam my eyes over the blood splattered leather. It's Zack's blood, but I suspect some of it could be mine too.

"You're not fit to wear that."

He glances at me. "They'll have to take my colours off my fucking dead body."

I smile at the thought.

"That might happen sooner than you think."

My attention goes back to the windscreen. I know with everything in my heart that even if my life ends at Sin's hands, even if he rips the last breath from my body, Ty and his brothers will end Sin's. They'll make him beg for it. They'll shed every piece of skin from his body, taking him to hell and bringing him back again.

He ignores my words and climbs out of the car, moving quickly around the front to come to the passenger door. When he opens it, my heart rate picks up speed. Grabbing my wrist, Sin drags me out of the car. I bang my knees against the dashboard trying to get free of the vehicle and cry out as he drops me to the ground, the concrete slamming into my shins.

"Get up," he growls, snagging my arm and tugging me up.

My legs are wobbly beneath me, a mix of my head wound

and my fear making them weak. I stumble, but he shoves the gun against my side and I try to keep traction.

Sin pulls the door, which is propped against the opening, aside and we step into the building.

It's dark and it takes my eyes a moment to adjust to the change. When it does a chill races through me. It's a large open space, with some rusted machinery in one corner and what looks like a few smaller rooms off the main space. The stench of something unpleasant tingles my nose, and I cover my face with the back of my hand as I'm shoved forward, stumbling over the debris littering the ground.

Sin leads us into a small room off the main floor and the smell is so intense now I gag.

"You puke, you'll be licking it up."

He shoves me forward and the stench hits the back of my throat, making me wretch again.

I freeze, my whole body beginning to shake as I take in the dirty mattress on the floor, a large brown patch on it. Blood. There are discarded medicine packages littering the floor at the far side of the mattress and old bloodied bandages. My gaze takes in the old food trays and used bottles of water and my stomach sinks.

Has he brought me to where he's been holed up since he went missing? Will Tyler even know where I am? I knew they were looking for Sin and coming up empty. Ty never spoke the words, never told me his worries, but I could see it in the tension around his eyes, the way anger surrounded him after every call about his brother.

As Sin pushes me further into the room, I see what is causing the smell. It's a half-decomposed body. It's slumped over on its side, although from the staining on the wall, it looks as if it was previously sitting against it.

My stomach twists and my eyes flare. I can't stop my feet from moving as bile crawls up my throat.

"Who's that?"

"Someone who was in my fucking way."

I step back right into the barrel of Sin's gun.

"Get on the mattress," he orders.

I shake my head. "I'm not getting on that."

He slams the gun handle down again, this time catching my cheek. I feel the skin split like an overripe peach and the warm gush of blood.

Ty's voice echoes in my head.

Play along until the men get to you...

I move to stand over the mattress, wrapping my arms around my waist.

"Lie down."

"No."

I can't do it. Not again.

"Lie down, Sash."

My face contorts into a mask of rage. "You'll have to kill me before I let you touch me like that again."

He reaches out and I flinch back, but he just tucks a piece of hair behind my ear. It's a strangely intimate gesture that has my senses on full alert. What the hell is he doing?

A strange look flickers in his eyes, almost like regret as he takes in the marks he's caused. His crazed eyes soften as his demons die down and he looks so much like the little boy he used to be.

"I always loved you," he surprises the fuck out of me by saying.

The blood all over my face suggests otherwise, but for once I keep my mouth shut.

"Why did Tyler get to have everything? The president's patch, the girl... What did I have?"

I narrow my eyes at him and pull away from his fingers.

"This is what this is all about? You're fucking jealous of

your brother? You raped me because you wanted what you couldn't have? Like a fucking prize?"

His brows draw together. "You should have been mine. I saw you first." He doesn't deny what he did.

I get in his face, not caring about the gun pointing at me and hiss, "I was never yours. I love Tyler. I'll always love him. You were my friend. That's all." My voice catches and I hate that it does.

I know I'm pushing him, but my anger is blowing. He destroyed my life because of some jealous notion he should have had what his brother had. He thinks because he saw me first that gave him some stupid claim to me? The thing is, Tyler would have given him anything in his power to give. He just couldn't give him what Sin desired most—me. I belonged to Ty the moment I first laid eyes on him. Even if he didn't want me, my heart would always have been his. I would always have been his.

Sin twitches, using the gun to scratch at his forehead as he closes his eyes. His motions are jerky and frantic. I can see he's losing control.

"Don't fucking say that, you bitch!"

His hand lashes out, catching my jaw. I stagger back, nearly losing my footing, but I manage to stay upright using the wall to steady myself.

"Why did you tell Rav we slept together? If you didn't want me, why tell him our secret?"

That's when reality hits me. He's beyond help. He's fucked up, his reality so messed up he doesn't know the truth.

"I've lost everything! I'll never be able to go home, I'm going to lose my kutte, probably my life."

My face burns, the skin feeling hot and tight. I peer up at him and let my mouth pull into a snarl.

"You fucking raped me!"

His brows draw together and he laughs, a low guttural sound that has my stomach flipping.

"I never raped you, you crazy bitch. You enjoyed it. Don't fucking lie and say you didn't."

Sickness crawls through me and my skin feels inked with dirt that no soap could ever remove.

"Enjoyed it? Was I enjoying it as I begged you to stop? As I screamed? As I pleaded with you not to fucking do it?" My chest heaves in harsh pants as I stare my demon, the monster of my nightmares, in the eyes. "You took what you wanted." I roll to my toes and get in his face, snapping, "No matter what you do to me, I'll never be yours. I'll never let you take anything from me again, you sick, disgusting bastard." I might not have a weapon, but I know the power of my words. "I will never, *ever* love you." Each word is low and wrapped in disgust.

Rage clouds his expression and fear rolls through me as his eyes glaze over. I see the demons resurface. I yelp as he manhandles me down onto the mattress. Clawing at his face, kicking at him, hitting him in the chest as hard as I can, I try to get him off me.

That last one seems to hurt him, because he snarls, "You fucking bitch. I'll make you mine," at me before he slams his fist into my face.

Dazed, I try to fight him, but he's stronger than I am, and I can do nothing as he gets me on my back.

The mattress springs stab into my spine as his weight comes down on top of me and my breath tears out of me in ragged pants.

"No!" I beat my hands against him as he tugs my borrowed joggers down past my knees. The oversized pants come down too easily, allowing him to spread my now bare legs with his knee between them. "Stop! Sin, stop!" I thrash, trying everything to stop from being sucked back into that place three years ago, but from the look in his eyes this just seems to excite him more. "James, please!" I sob out his real name, but it doesn't penetrate through the darkness swirling around him.

He holds my wrists over my head in one hand while the other moves to my breast. I taste vomit in my mouth as he squeezes it.

I fight with everything I have, but he's sitting on my hips, stopping me from moving.

Then I hear it. A sound that is like a fanfare of relief. The sound of pipes rumbling and the unmistakable roar of multiple Harley engines.

A single tear falls down my cheek as his name falls from my lips in a soft whisper. "Tyler."

29

RAVAGE

I HONESTLY THOUGHT he wouldn't be here, that I'd be wrong. When I storm into the warehouse, my brothers at my back, the last thing I expect to see in that filthy blood-soaked room is my woman underneath my brother, a pair of my joggers around her ankles, a gun pressed to her temple, and her face covered in blood.

I can see the fear in her eyes as they dart back and forth, the tension in every line of her body.

My only thought is am I too late. Did he rape her again? I can't see any sign of obvious trauma, apart from the mess of her face. I do notice her eyes are a little heavy, as if she's struggling to keep focused, but there's also relief in them and love. That cuts me open.

I'm aware of my brothers at my back, and hear their guns cocking as I step closer to Sin. Fire scorches a path through my gut. He has no right to touch her. He never did.

My gaze slides to Sin and I curl my mouth up into a snarl. I watch his eyes widen. He's never had this look focused on him. It's one I usually reserve for our enemies. He drags her up, pulling her in front of him like a shield and my heart goes wild.

"Take your fucking hands off her."

Sin cocks his head at me. He doesn't look great either. His face is a mass of darkly yellowing bruises. My heart starts to canter in my chest as I stare at my little brother, a man who is now threatening to take everything important from me. His time is up, but looking at him now, it's hard not to see the little boy I protected from our mother, from Johns looking to climb into his bed. All I see now is blood, pain, betrayal and an enemy.

"I'm not fucking stupid. I let her go and you'll kill me." The high lilt of his voice scares me. "You let fucking snatch come between us," he growls.

I tense. He's unpredictable right now and that could get Sasha hurt, but my anger can't be curtailed, so his words piss me off.

"She ain't fucking snatch and you know it."

I feel my brothers shifting behind me at my back and I meet Sasha's eyes, trying to tell her without words that I'm going to fix this. I'm going to make it right.

I have no idea how, but I will.

"Let her go, Sin," Nox says. "This is the end of the fucking road for you."

"I know what the end of the road looks like when it comes to the Sons. I'll take my chances."

"You had every chance until you put your hands on my old lady, before you took something from her you had no right to take," I hiss. "Die now, die later. Either way, you ain't walking out of this fucking building alive."

"You'd kill your own blood? You always saved me, Rav. Can you really kill me? Your little brother? It's always been us against the fucking world."

His words sink in, grabbing hold of me and messing with

my head. The image of him young and scared flits behind my eyelids. Then the images turn to Sash and what he did to her, what he took. I shake my head. The brother I knew died a long time ago. Now, an evil piece of shit has taken his place.

"You raped her, you sick fuck. You think I can even bear to look at your fucking face knowing that?"

Sasha's eyes move to Nox and she blinks a couple of times. She jabs her elbow back, catching Sin in the side. He doubles over as she flattens herself to the floor.

Two loud pops of gunfire fill the space, deafening me for a second. I move without thought, reaching out for Sash and dragging her across the floor towards me. I'm sure I scrape up her legs, but that's the least of my concerns.

Is she shot? Did he shoot her? I don't see blood apart from the shit coating her face.

Sin staggers back, clutching his shoulder. Red pours between his fingers as my brothers surround him. My real brothers. Sin might have been my brother by blood, but not where it matters.

I ignore my brother as the lads surround him, taking him down to his knees, and focus on Sasha. Certain she wasn't caught in the crossfire, my hands cup her jaw, my heart racing as I try to touch her without hurting her.

"Baby, you're safe now."

She peers into my face, her eyes a little glassy and I see tears welling. I probably shouldn't, but I can't stop from pressing my mouth to her swollen, split lips. She doesn't stop me, kissing me back as if her life depends on it.

"I knew you'd come," she whispers when I pull back, our foreheads touching.

"Always."

And I mean that. She's mine and I'll die to protect her.

"Can you stand?"

Sash nods and lets me help her to her feet. She fumbles to

pull her joggers up and then she turns to Sin. I brace, not sure what she's going to do. She pulls her foot back and kicks him between the legs so hard I wince. His pained groan echoes around the room.

"Rot in hell," she growls at him.

Sin doubles over clutching his balls. "You bitch!" he screams, but is cut off by a fist to the gut from Fury.

I signal to the doc to follow me, and my arm wraps around Sasha's shoulders as I lead her outside.

The fresh air hits me like an anvil to the face. I breathe it in, feeling relief pass through me as realisation dawns that my woman is okay.

Ignoring Whizz, I take Sasha's head in my hands once more, knowing I've got to ask the question.

"Did he...?" I break off unable to bring myself to imagine that my brother raped my girl again.

Sasha shakes her head, her fingers sifting through my hair. "No. You got here before it happened." She strokes my face.

I dip my head to hers, letting out a shuddering breath. "Thank fuck."

I turn back, taking in the injuries to her face, cataloguing each one. Sin will pay for every hurt he put on her. For every mark she has, he'll pay double.

My gaze slides over her shoulder to Whizz.

"Take Sasha back to the clubhouse."

"You got it, Prez."

I turn to Sash. "You can ride?"

"Come with me." Her hands fist into my kutte, whitening around the leather. Sasha isn't the type to ask for anything, so I grit my teeth, not in anger, but because I hate disappointing her. I'd give her the fucking moon if she asked, but not this. I can't give her this.

"You know I can't."

She knows how the club works, what happens to men who cross us.

"Killing Sin won't make any of this better." I hear the plea in her voice, and as much as it kills me to ignore it, I do.

I kiss her. "Go with Whizz."

"Tyler…"

"Go with Whizz," I growl. "I'll be back soon."

She looks as though she's going to argue with me again, but she nods and the heavy weight in my chest loosens slightly. I hand her my helmet and help her put it on. She winces as the side touches her face and my anger flares. I'm going to gut Sin for every mark he's put on her skin.

Her eyes stay locked on mine as Whizz walks over to his bike and climbs on. Under normal circumstances, my woman on the back of anyone's bike but mine would have me tearing up the city, but she needs to get back to the safety of the clubhouse fast, and I trust Whizz. Besides, she needs to be looked over by him to make sure she doesn't have any serious injuries. Her face is covered in so much blood I can't tell where her wounds start and end.

Sasha swallows hard as she glances at me, then climbs up behind Whizz, her hands going behind her back to hold the handrail. Whizz peers at me before starting up his engine, giving me a nod to tell me he has it covered. Then he peels out of there like the devil is on his heels.

Nox walks out, his eyes as dangerous as mine as he watches the Harley take off.

"I spoke to Lucy. She'll stay with Lily."

I nod tersely. I don't ask how he's got her number or why. I don't care.

I watch the horizon as Sasha and Whizz get further away before I move back into the building. The stone wrapped around my heart hardens as I stride back into the room and find my brother kneeling in the middle of the floor, his head

189

bowed. His kutte is sitting on the floor next to him, leaving him in just his tee and jeans. He looks strange, naked.

With a calm I don't feel, I bend down and pull my knife from my boot, slowly pulling it free of the sheath.

I stare at my brother's bent head, my heart starting to race in my chest. This is it. This is the end of the line. I've killed many men, but never have any of those deaths bothered me. This one is going to cut me up to my last breath.

Sin peers up through his shaggy hair and I don't see the man who raped my woman for a moment. I see the little boy I raised and kept safe, the kid who always looked to me for protection, the kid I loved.

Fuck. It's like an axe to my heart. I can barely draw air as I shift the knife in my hand.

Then I remember Sasha's joggers around her ankles, the blood on her face and my mouth pulls into a snarl.

"Time to pay for your sins."

I stab the knife into his shoulder, ignoring his scream.

30

SASHA

THE RIDE back to the clubhouse feels like it takes forever. As we ride, all I can think about is the look on Ty's face. This is killing him.

By the time the building comes into sight, my face is on fire and my head is throbbing. I'm barely hanging on behind Whizz.

He stops right outside the back entrance, not bothering to pull into a space and cuts the engine. I climb off his Harley, my legs shaking beneath me, and I have to use the back of the bike to steady myself.

"You doing okay there?" Whizz asks, switching into doctor mode as he eyes me clinically.

"I'm a little dizzy," I admit.

I'm a lot dizzy. My head is rolling and nausea is swirling in my gut.

"Let's take a look at you."

He takes my arm and gently leads me into the building. As we move into the common room, I brace, expecting to see blood and Zack's body, but as my eyes stray to where he fell, there's no sign of the murdered prospect. There's no blood stains and the floor is spotless. There's no sign of what happened here only a few hours ago and if it wasn't for the slight smell of bleach hanging in the air and tickling my nose, I wouldn't believe this was the scene of a murder.

I shouldn't be surprised. The club is really good at clean up. I just hope they give Zack a proper send off. The kid was stupid, but he didn't deserve to be put down like a dog.

Whizz moves me over to a table and orders me to sit. I sink down onto the chair as he disappears to get his medical bag.

I can't stop from glancing around the room and as I do a shiver works up my spine. This was where my nightmare began, but at least this time I was saved. Last time as I lay beneath Sin, fighting him off, I prayed to every God I could think of to be saved, but help never came. Today, Tyler rode in like my white knight on a steel horse, and I'll never forget that. The fear in his eyes when Sin was holding me was something I've never seen before, but it was there, mixing with the anger. What struck me harder, what ripped my heart open, was the hurt. I know Ty believed me from the moment he found out what happened, but seeing the truth with his own eyes was worse than any bullet could do to him. Ty is president of the Sons for a reason, but what a lot of people don't know is that he loves as hard as he fights. A brother turning on the club was bad enough—everyone felt that knife to the heart—but his own brother, his blood, the boy he grew up protecting all his life, that did something dark to a person. It will twist him up.

I rub my hands up my cold arms. Riding in just a tee, even in the British summer, leaves me feeling chilled, but it's not the weather that has me shivering. Coming face to face with my nightmare, fighting him again, taking on my demons leaves me a trembling mess. For three years, I dreamed of what I'd do if I saw Sin again. I dreamed of all the things I'd say to him, do to him for ruining my life, for making me believe my family would turn their back on me. It didn't play out how I imagined and I don't feel better for it. Now, I worry what all this will do to Tyler.

Killing Sin won't change what happened. It won't repair the past three years, but it will shred Ty. I wish he would have listened to my pleas and walked away, not tarnished his soul with this death, but I know he would never be able to rest knowing his brother still breathed free air.

I just hope this isn't going to destroy him, destroy us.

Whizz steps back into the room, carrying a leather bag that he heaves onto the adjacent table. He opens it up and pulls out some supplies.

"I just want to check your pupils," he tells me.

I shrug, not caring what he does to me. All my thoughts are on Tyler and what he's doing right now. I jiggle my leg up and down as Whizz shines a light in my eyes, wincing at the brightness.

"Any nausea?"

"Yeah."

"Headache?"

"I got hit in the head with a gun. What do you think?"

His mouth pulls into a tight line and his eyes narrow at my words.

"Fucking Sin," he hisses out.

Warmth floods me at his show of emotion. These men who I turned my back on have welcomed me back without question—something Sin told me would never happen. I hate myself for listening to him.

"I'm okay," I tell him, my voice soft.

"You're not okay. Not even a little. Your face is a mess and I'm pretty sure you have a concussion. Nothing about this is okay."

I place a hand on Whizz's arm.

"Whizz, really, I'm okay. It's Rav I'm worried about."

"He'll be fine."

I arch my brow at him. "You really believe that?"

He peers at me for a moment before he mutters out a, "Yeah," but there's no strength to his words. I can see the worry for his president.

He doesn't elaborate and I don't push him for details. He moves to his bag and pulls out some gauze and saline. For the next ten minutes he cleans the blood off my face then he stitches two gashes on my head and face. He hands me a bottle of Jack to numb the pain, but it doesn't do shit. It hurts like hell, and I have to bite my swollen lip to keep from crying out. Whizz works fast, methodically and when he's done, he pulls off his latex gloves and drops his hands to his hips.

"You're going to have a fuck ton of bruising, but hopefully those two wounds won't scar too badly. You can sleep, but I'll be in every hour to make sure you're okay." He hands me a couple of pills. "For the pain."

Sleep isn't going to happen. I'm wired and on edge waiting for news from Ty.

"I want to get back to the hospital."

"You need to take care of you."

"My daughter—"

"Will be fine."

I want to argue further, but I'm so tired I doubt I would be any use to Lil right now anyway.

"Zack…" I murmur, my gaze straying to where he was gunned down. "What happened to him?"

Whizz scrubs a hand over his clean jaw and sighs. "Go and get some rest."

"Whizz."

"It's club business, darlin'."

He doesn't say anything else. He doesn't need to. "Club

business" says everything. He's not going to say a word about it.

I push up from the chair, wobbling slightly. Whizz reaches out to steady me.

"You okay there?"

"Yeah, just finding my feet," I say on a smile that is forced.

Whizz considers me for a moment, then says, "It's good to have you back, Sash. Club wasn't the same with you gone."

Warmth spreads through me at his words. "It's good to be back."

Whizz helps me upstairs and leaves me in Tyler's room. It's weird being back here. This morning, everything was so perfect. Now, everything feels tainted. Ty's tee I borrowed is covered in blood, so I pull it over my head and find a clean one in his drawers. This time when I see the knives, my stomach twists. I can't even think about what he's doing to Sin right now without feeling nausea. I don't care about him. I hope he rots in hell, but I do care about Ty and how this will stain him afterwards. Killing his brother isn't something he can just forget about once it's done. It will be like a knife to the heart for him. I wish he had come back with me and let the brothers deal with Sin, but I grew up in this world. I know that isn't how it works. For once, I wish I was an innocent to all this. I wish I didn't know what my man is doing.

I climb into the bed we shared this morning, the sheets still smelling of Tyler and snuggle down. I'm exhausted, my body bone weary. I reach over to his side of the bed, wishing he was here with me, wishing I could take this burden from him.

I doze for a while, but Whizz wakes me an hour later to check my eyes again. He does this over the next several hours, and in the end, I give up on sleeping.

I'm staring up at the ceiling, my mind blank of thoughts when I hear the door go again and I groan. It can't have been an hour already. I shift my gaze towards the door, intending to give Whizz a piece of my mind, but it's not Whizz standing in the doorway. It's a blood-soaked Tyler.

I sit up fast, pushing the covers down my body and swallow back bile as I take in the blood coating his face and hands, over his tee. His kutte looks clean, though.

I try to muffle my gasp as I climb out of bed and move towards him slowly. He doesn't say a word, just watches me like a rabid animal, waiting to pounce. His eyes are wilder than I've ever seen. It's like Ty has disappeared and Ravage, the man that people fear, is in his place.

I approach him cautiously, not sure where his head is at. "Tyler?"

His eyes raise to mine and he mutters, "It's done."

My stomach twists at his words.

"Let's get you cleaned up."

I watch as his body tenses, stopping me from moving any closer. His hand reaches out, but something flickers in his eyes and he drops it before making contact.

Then he growls out, "He'll never fucking touch you again."

RAVAGE

I FEEL numb as I stand in front of Sash. I knew there was darkness in me, a darkness that was so vile it could never be redeemed, but I had no idea how far down the hole I was willing to go until today.

I stare down at the blood coating my hands, blood that belongs to my brother and feel nausea climb up my throat. I need to get clean, but I can't make my legs move.

Sasha takes my head in her hands, lifting my chin. It takes everything I have not to flinch back from her touch.

"We need to… wash you." Her voice cracks with emotion.

I want to reassure her, but my words stick in my throat. I don't want my filth touching her. I told her he would never touch her again and that includes his blood I'm soaked in.

I let her lead me into the bathroom. I blink as I catch my reflection in the mirror, the blood coating me a reminder of what I've done. I can't meet her eyes as she strips me like I'm a child and my thoughts empty as I stand there, dick swinging in the breeze as she turns on the water.

I'm empty. I wish I could feel anger that my brother put

me in this position, but right now I'm not capable of feeling anything.

I know it had to be done, but taking his life wasn't easy. My skin crawls with dirt and I feel the weight of my actions pushing down on my shoulders.

Sasha guides me under the spray and removes her own clothes before stepping into the cubicle with me. Her eyes dart to my face as she squeezes some shower gel onto her hand and starts to wash me with a gentleness I don't deserve.

I can't bear it. I don't want her to see me like this.

I grab her wrists, halting her.

"Stop."

"Ty..."

"Enough!" I growl.

Hurt flashes in her eyes, but I ignore it, ignore that I'm the cause of it.

"Get out."

"Don't do this."

"Get the fuck out."

Her eyes flare, but she climbs out of the shower, grabbing a towel from the rail. I watch as she wraps it around herself before snatching her clothes off the floor and heading into the bedroom.

Once she's gone, I'm able to breathe freely for the first time since I delivered the final blow to my brother.

I want to scream at her to come back, but then I see the rose-tinted water and the truth of the man I am.

She's been through hell, too, but I can't bear to have her looking at me with so much love. Not when I don't deserve it from her.

I scrub at my hands, at my face, trying to clean myself, but no amount of washing is going to clean this sin from me.

I killed my brother.

There's a special place in hell reserved for me, just as

there is for him. Sin's not innocent in this. He brought us to this place and I hate him for that. I hate that he forced my hand. My brother had to die, he had to pay for his crimes, but I wish I hadn't been the one who had to do it.

I wash quickly and methodically, scrubbing the blood from my face, from my hands, from every inch of me. I scrub my skin until it's raw, but I can still feel his blood on me, I can still hear his voice begging me, see the tears that coated his cheeks. The look in his eyes as I delivered the final blow will haunt me for the rest of my days.

As the water starts to go cold, I force myself out from under the spray. I don't have any clean clothes in the bathroom, so I wrap a towel around my waist and step into the bedroom. I expect Sasha to be gone, but she's sitting on the edge of the bed, her wet hair hanging in loose strands around her battered face.

When she raises soft eyes to me, I feel my heart shatter into a thousand pieces.

"Don't push me away."

It's a plea, but I ignore it. If I go to her, I'll lose my composure and I can't let that happen. I won't let my anger, my frustration, my despair spill out on her. I want to lose myself in her, but I'll never take her in anger. I'll never use her body for an escape.

"I've got shit to do."

My words come out terser than I intend and I hate myself for making her pull her walls back up with me after I spent so long breaking them down, but I can't stay with her tonight. I can't lie next to her and pretend everything is okay, that I don't have a hole left behind in my heart from my brother's demise. My body is at war. I fucking hate him. I would send him to hell every day for what he did, to keep her safe. Yet it goes against everything that's ingrained in me. I'm supposed to protect him. It's hard not to remember the little kid who climbed into my bed when Johns came knocking. He looked at me like I was his hero. Today, I lost that. The only thing I'd seen in his eyes was fear.

I quickly pull on a pair of boxers, followed by a pair of clean jeans. I find a shirt in the drawer and shrug into it, all the while feeling her eyes on me. My head is a fucked-up mess, a jumble of thoughts I can't sort through and right now, I just need time to think. I can't do that with Sasha in my space. I'm too on edge, knowing I can fall off that ledge at any time.

"I'll be back later," I mutter, then step out of the room, pulling the door shut behind me. I half expect her to come after me, but she doesn't.

I head down to my office. I can't face the brothers, not yet. Dragging open my top drawer, I take out the bottle of Scotch I keep there and swig straight from it, relishing the burn as it hits my throat. I knock back half the bottle before I come back up for air, then I tip my head back against the headrest of the chair and stare at the ceiling.

It feels wrong to mourn a piece of shit rapist, but that's not who I'm grieving for. It's the little boy I raised and protected over the years. It's the kid who looked to me to make things right. It's the kid I always took care of.

I wanted desperately to see that kid in the eyes of the monster kneeling at my feet, but he was long gone, until the very end, when he whispered my name.

Fuck.

Sin was a new kind of animal, one who saw nothing wrong with taking what he shouldn't. He had his own demons, ones that could never be exorcised. There was no coming back from what he did. There was no amount of talking it out that would fix it, no amount of forgiveness that could put it right. What he did was unforgivable. He ruined Sasha's life. Mine too. He took my daughter from me, he made Sasha feel she had to raise that kid alone. If it wasn't for her getting sick I might never have known my child. That gores me. I want to be a good dad. Better than mine ever was, but I have so much dark in me I'm not sure that's possible. They'd probably be better off without me in their lives, but I'm a selfish bastard. I can't give them up.

He also took the woman I love from me. No one ever understood me or loved me the way Sasha did. Losing that nearly destroyed me. Sin watched me suffer through that loss, commiserated with me, told me to get over the bitch. All the while he knew he was the reason she was gone.

The lies, the betrayal is what guts me the most. I didn't deserve that from him. I sacrificed so much for Sin over the years. I gave up pieces of myself to keep him safe. How could he grow to hate me so much?

Memories of his last moments flash through my mind, the blood, his pleading. I take another drink, trying to block it out, but no amount of booze is going to fix this.

I killed my brother.

And there's no coming back from that.

SASHA

I WAIT for Tyler to come back to the room, but after a few hours, it's obvious he's not going to. I've chewed my nails down to the beds, my stomach churning as I stare at the door, willing it to open, willing him to step through it. He doesn't.

I can't stand it any longer. I push to my feet, tugging up my borrowed joggers. I'm not going to let him push me away. I refuse to let him destroy what we've been building together since I came back. I love him, and he needs me, but he's hurting, which is why he's being this way. Ty might act tough, but he's not completely unfeeling. He saved me, and now it's time to do the same for him. Now it's time for me to be the one who bears the weight of his demons.

Barefooted, I wander down the corridors and make my way towards the executive officers' offices. I expect to find Ty holed up down here, but when I knock on the door, I get no response. I wait half a second before I push the handle down and peer around the frame.

Empty.

He's not here.

Anxiety pierces me. Would he have taken off? Where the fuck would he have gone?

I head for the common room and as soon as I push inside, I see red. Ty is here, sitting at the bar, a half-empty bottle of Scotch in front of him and some skanky redhead has her mucky paws all over him. He's not paying her any attention, his eyes unfocused across the room, staring into space, but he's also not pushing her away, which pisses me the hell off. He's mine, and I'll fight any bitch who tries to claim otherwise.

I barely notice the other brothers sitting around the room. My attention is locked on my man.

I start towards him, but a hand is suddenly wrapped around my bicep like a vice. I flinch instinctively, old habits hard to break, until I realise the hand belongs to Nox. He doesn't let me go, but he does loosen his hold slightly.

"Go back upstairs, Sash."

If he thinks he can tell me what to do, he's crazy.

"He's mine," I hiss.

His expression hardens at my words.

"Rav's in a bad way."

I won't be taken for a ride. He wants loyalty from me? Well, I expect that shit in return.

I roll to my toes and get in his face, my anger flaring. "He needs me, not some fucking club bitch. I can take anything he throws at me."

I shrug him off and he lets me go. I'm practically spitting fire by the time I reach the bar.

"Take your hands off him," I snarl at her.

She arches a delicate brow at me, but doesn't remove her touch.

"Who the hell do you think you are?" Red growls at me, her hand moving up to Ty's shoulder.

I don't think. I snatch her hand and bend it up her back until she's dancing on her toes to try to alleviate the pressure.

"Get it into your head. That man there is mine. You don't touch him, you don't fuck him, you don't try to get your dirty claws into him. You do and we're going to have a problem."

I let her go with a shove and she stumbles on her high heels. "Rav, are you going to let this bitch talk to me like this?" she demands in a whiny voice that grates on my nerves.

I fold my arms over my chest and peer down at my man.

"She's my fucking old lady," Tyler snaps out, although his words are slurred together. "I would listen to her if I were you."

"Rav!" the redhead complains.

"Leave me the fuck alone, Melody," he mutters.

I watch as the bunny sashays off with a huff, trying to sink her teeth into a new victim—Levi—but he brushes her off too, too focused on what's happening with his president.

I turn my attention back to Tyler. He takes a long swig of his drink. "Go away, Sash."

His words flay me. Agony lances through my chest, knowing everyone is watching us, but I can't show weakness now. I need to be the woman they all remember—Priest's daughter. She's not the kind of woman who will beg.

My heart breaks as I grind out, "You don't want me? Fine. I'm gone. I'm not going to beg for scraps."

As I start to turn, he grabs my arm, stopping me. "You ain't leaving."

"Fuck that, Ty. I'm not some club bunny you can blow off when you get bored of me."

His glassy gaze moves towards me and I see pain reflected in his eyes. My anger simmers down and I swallow past the lump in my throat.

"I'm yours. Come back to the room. Let me help you."

"You can't. You can't undo what I've done." His throat works as he says it and my heart breaks for him.

"No, I can't, but I'll take that anger, anything you throw at me. I can handle it." He doesn't reply, so I add, "Come to bed, please."

He shakes his head. "Can't."

I let out a breath and use the only other weapon in my arsenal. "I'm going to the hospital to see *our* daughter."

He flinches at my words and I see a little of the ice start to crack.

"A brother will take you. You don't go alone."

The argument sits on the tip of my tongue, but I swallow it back. He's not thinking straight and I get that, but as with Sin, I know my words can be weapons.

"I love you," I tell him, my words wobbling. "Don't let him destroy us. Don't give him that power."

He raises his head and his eyes bore into mine, as if seeing me for the first time. He's not drunk, but he has checked out. I don't know how to reach him.

"I killed James." It's weird to hear him call Sin by his real name and it makes it more real.

"I know." Tears well in my eyes.

"He needed to die."

"Yeah."

His face contorts into a broken snarl. "I can't stand it."

I don't care who is watching, I wrap my arms around him and burrow my head into his chest.

"He wasn't James. He hasn't been for a long time. He wasn't the brother you remember."

He kisses my forehead. "Yeah."

"Sin was broken. His head too messed up. He made those choices. That's on him. Not you."

Ty slides off the stool. "Bed."

Relief floods me and as he staggers, I reach out to catch

him. He nearly knocks me on my arse with his huge bulk. Then Nox and Daimon are there, taking a side of him. These men are his brothers. Not Sin. There was no loyalty there, no love. Sin hated him for things that were out of his control. Jealousy is a fickle bitch and it got him killed.

Day and Nox help him upstairs, mostly carrying him as they move.

I open the door and get out of the way as they dump him on the bed. He flops back, his unfocused gaze on the ceiling.

I walk the two guys back to the door.

"Thanks."

"You need help getting him settled?" Day asks.

"Do you think he'd appreciate you tucking him in?"

Daimon grunts in amusement.

"I've got it from here," I assure them.

"Sash," Nox says my name quietly. "You're okay, right?"

I nod, my smile thin. "Yeah."

"Just know that fucker paid for what he did to you, but doing it fucked with Rav's head. He's going to need some time to wrap his mind around what he did."

I give him a thin smile, feeling my heart shattering at his words. Ty did this for me and now he's hurting. That cuts deep. "He'll get through it."

"Yeah, he will." He raps his knuckles on the door frame and pushes back. "You need anything, you call."

"Thanks."

I shut the door and for a moment, I stare at the wood, trying to gather my thoughts. I have no idea what to say to Tyler to fix this. I don't know if this can ever be fixed, which is why I didn't want him to do it.

I move over to the bed and peer down at him. Then without a word, I start to unlace his left boot. I tug it off his foot and move to the right. Both boots off, I move to his belt and undo it. He doesn't move, his eyes still focused on the ceiling as I manage to wrestle his jeans down past his hips.

Once he's free of the denim, I move to his top half. "You're going to have to help me here, Ty," I mutter.

He doesn't speak or move. With a sigh, I crawl onto the bed and lie down next to him. Then I wrap my arm around him, nuzzling up against his side.

"I know it doesn't mean much right now, but thank you for what you did."

He shifts beneath me and his hand moves to stroke over my hair. The tension in my chest starts to loosen.

I lean up and press my mouth to his, needing to show him without words how much. He stiffens at first, but then he relaxes into the kiss. I take the lead, swiping my tongue along the seam of his lips, begging for entry. He gives it to me and as soon as I'm inside, I caress his tongue.

His hand tangles in my hair, holding me in place as he takes my mouth like a starving man eating his last meal. My heart is racing, pounding so hard I'm sure he can feel it against him. I should be terrified of taking this step, but I'm not. This is Tyler, not Sin, and I want this. I want him.

He shoves my tee up to my armpits, taking a moment to appreciate my uncovered tits, glad I'm not wearing a bra, before the garment is dragged over my head. I lean forwards, putting my nipple in reach of his mouth and he leans up taking it. A shiver runs through me as his tongue swipes over the hard, little bud and I close my eyes, feeling the sensations running through my body.

He plays with both nipples, alternating between the two as he devours each nub in turn. Within minutes, I'm writhing on top of him, between my legs dampening with every passing swipe of his tongue. I pant, my breath ripping out of me. I never thought sex could feel good again, but being on top is giving me a sense of control, I need to do this.

"Pull down your joggers," he orders.

My pussy throbs at his words and I do as he asks, shaking them off my ankles.

"Lose the underwear."

His bossiness has my mouth drying out. I shimmy out of the clean boxers I borrowed from Ty after the shit with Sin. I couldn't bring myself to wear anything that he touched, so Ty let me raid his drawers after I showered.

I toss the boxers on the floor behind me while he sits up and pulls off his kutte and tee, leaving him in just his underwear.

I sit back on his torso, my bare pussy against his stomach. His fingers move to my hips and he tugs me towards him. I move up his body as he directs me until I'm sitting over his face. Then his tongue dips out and goes between my folds. I gasp, my back arching as electricity flashes through my pussy. He doesn't stop. His tongue goes to work, brushing back and forth over my sensitive clit. Clinging to the headboard, I try not to drop my weight onto him, even though my legs feel weak.

I can feel my orgasm building as he keeps eating my pussy, his fingers digging into my thighs to pull me closer. I'm barely able to breathe as sensations wash through me that I haven't felt in three years, that I thought I'd never feel again. With Tyler, I feel safe. I feel in control.

I lose that control as stars flicker behind my eyes and my pussy pulses in time with my racing heart. I moan his name as he takes me over the edge and it takes everything I have not to collapse on top of him.

I take a moment to recover, then move to his boxers. Slowly, I slide them down his legs, releasing his hard cock. I want it inside me.

Ty grabs my wrist before my fingers can wrap around his length.

"You don't have to."

I peer at my man with my pussy juice shimmering on his beard. Heat pools in my belly at the look he's giving me and my pussy throbs.

"I want to."

His fingers release their hold and I wrap my own around his shaft, slowly pulling and twisting up and down it. He shifts, groaning a little at the movement, his legs widening as I move my hand. We keep our eyes locked on each other, electric energy bouncing between us. He's my soulmate. We fit each other perfectly. He's the only man I'll ever want or need. With Ty, I feel safe, loved, whole. He doesn't make me feel dirty or wrong. For the first time in years, the dirt covering me is being washed away.

When he's hard, I sit myself so I'm hovering over his cock and meet his eyes. I see trust and love there. I hope the same thing is reflected in my eyes because I do love this man and I absolutely trust him.

He reaches into his bedside table and pulls out a condom. I take it from him, opening the wrapper before I slide it down the length of his shaft. I don't miss the twitching of his thighs as I scrape my fingers over his sensitive length.

He peers up at me and I see the question in his eyes, which are no longer dull and unseeing, but bright and focused.

Do you want this?

In answer, I swipe the head of his engorged cock through my folds and then slowly lower myself onto the shaft. I hold my breath as his girth stretches my pussy and keep my eyes locked on him, reminding myself this is Tyler, not Sin, that I want this. It's easier when he's looking at me like I'm his reason for breathing right now. The connection we always had is there still, stronger, more vibrant than ever. We both survived hell and came out the other side.

When he's seated fully inside me, I let out a little whimper. A rush of feelings washes over me. Front and centre is anxiety, but I push it aside, and focus on the man beneath me. He swallows hard, and I can see it's taking every ounce of self-control not to move his hips.

Slowly, I pull myself up off him nearly to the tip and then push back down on him. Tyler tries to give me the control I need, but he's not built to be a passive passenger either. His hips start to move and he pushes deep inside me before pulling back, over and over. I let him take control, my hands pressed against his chest as I move in time with his rhythm. My breaths are coming in sharp little pants now. His hands grip my hips as I move against him, rotating my pelvis to drive him deeper inside me.

My orgasm hits first, and I moan as I jerk on his cock. Then I feel him twitch beneath me as he shoots his load into the condom. I collapse onto his chest, feeling him slip out of me, hating the loss of him, but when his arms wrap around me, I snuggle into him.

"I love you, Tyler. Don't ever forget that."

There's a long moment of silence. "I love you too, baby. Always."

RAVAGE

Sasha dozes for a while after we fuck, and I leave her to sleep. It's good to see. She needs the rest. She's been working so hard, taking care of Lily-May and trying to work through the nightmares my brother left behind. I doubt she's had any peaceful nights for a long time.

I shouldn't have let things go as far as they did between us, but we both needed each other. I wanted to take things slow with her, get her comfortable with me again. I never wanted to use her body to soothe my own pain, but I couldn't stop myself from taking what was offered. I needed her more than I've ever needed anyone. I still need her. Sasha does what I can't do for myself. She appeases the savage beast inside me, makes me feel less broken.

Taking her pussy, connecting our bodies, helped put some of my monsters back in their boxes. I feel level-headed again, surer of my decisions. I know it'll take me a long time to come to terms with what I did to my brother. I know I'll feel the pain until my last breath is taken, but I know deep down it had to happen. Sasha was right when she said he wasn't the James I remembered. Something had changed in him, twisting his mind. As long as he was breathing, Sin would continue to be a danger to Sasha. I know he would have killed her; that his obsession ran too deep for any other outcome. I couldn't have him out there like that. Sasha would never be able to move on.

I know I can't have the old Sasha back. I'm not the same man she remembers. She's also scarred by her past. She'll have to carry those marks with her, just as I will, but she is regaining some of that previous fire I loved about her. I can see it in her eyes, in the way she looks at me. Every piece of her I put back is redemption. I should never have trusted anyone else with the most important thing in my world. I won't make that mistake again.

I peer at her face, dark purple bruises starting to appear along her cheeks, and my jaw clenches. She got hurt on my watch, and that's something I'll never forgive myself for. I'll spend a lifetime making that up to her.

"Ty."

She stirs and I watch as her beautiful eyes find mine. Her smile slays me. How did I go without her this long? How did I let her walk away?

I watch as she struggles to sit up in the bed, the sheet dropping to reveal dark nipples. My eyes slide to them before moving up to her face.

"Sleep okay?"

"Yeah. What time is it?"

"After seven."

Her eyes flare and she pushes back the blankets. "We should get back to the hospital. Lily—"

"Will be fine with Lucy and Kyle."

She leans over in the bed and presses her mouth to mine before she says, "I need to see my baby."

How can I refuse her or Lily-May anything?

"Get dressed."

I watch as she climbs out of bed and pulls on her jeans from the other night. Getting out too, I pull on my own boxers and jeans before moving over to the dresser. I find two clean tees in the drawer and toss her one, shrugging into the other myself. The tee, an old Harley one, swims on her, but seeing her in my clothes makes my cock twitch. Possessiveness washes through me and I move over to her, my hands skimming up the back of the tee to the bare skin of her back as I crash my mouth onto hers.

I feel her melt against me as I deepen the kiss, but I pull away before I get too carried away and we end up in bed again.

Breathless, she peers up at me. "Thank you."

"For what?"

"Treating me like I'm normal."

"You are normal." I brush her hair back from her face. "Let's go and see our girl."

She nods, and I see the reluctance to release me in her expression as she pulls away from me to continue dressing. I like that it's there.

Snagging my kutte off the floor where it was dropped earlier, I shrug into it and settle it into place. Then I hold my hand out to Sasha.

She takes it without hesitation and I lead her out of the clubhouse. I don't take her to my bike, instead leading her to one of the pool cars we use when we need four wheels instead of two. She'd probably be okay on the back of a bike, but Whizz also said she has a concussion. I'm not risking her falling off.

Sasha doesn't question it as she climbs into the car and waits for me to take off my kutte and turn it inside out before I get into the cage. I don't ride in cages with my colours on display ever.

As we drive, she tells me stories about Lily-May. I listen to her words, feeling pride bubbling in my stomach.

When we reach the hospital, I can see the tension rolling through my woman, the eagerness to get to our daughter. I feel it too. Together, we walk into the building and head for the children's department.

As we approach the room, Kyle rises from his seat outside the door. His eyes go to Sasha's face, and I see him taking in the bruises and cuts with curiosity.

"Everything been okay?" Sash demands.

He nods and we push into the room. Lucy straightens in the chair at the side of the bed and I clock the moment she sees Sasha's face. Her expression moves from smiley to downright homicidal, as her eyes lock onto my face.

"What the fuck happened?"

The unspoken insinuation that I did it has me growling under my breath. I'd never lay a finger on Sasha like that. That she would accuse me pisses me off as much as it impresses me. Not many women, fuck, not many men, would stand up to me like that. Sash has a good friend here.

"What the fuck are you accusing me of?" My anger flares. I'm guilty of many things and I've done a lot of shit that has stained my soul over the years, but I've never raised a hand to a woman and I'm not about to start.

"He didn't do anything to me," Sasha says to Lucy. I like her taking my corner. "It was Sin."

Lucy's eyes widen, a ripple of shock going through her.

"Sin did this?"

"I'm okay," she assures her, her hand resting on her arm. "Ty wouldn't hurt me, Luce. Not ever."

"Sorry," she mutters an apology.

I should be the bigger person and accept it, but I shrug.

"Don't give a fuck what you or anyone else thinks of me."

The only people I do care about are Sasha and my daughter.

I move over to the cot bed and peer down at my kid, my heart cracking open for her. She's perfect. I don't deserve such innocence, such purity in my life. Not with my filthy history, but I can't bring myself to walk away. I want this. I want the family. I need it more than ever now.

"Hey, baby girl." I move my finger over her cheek like I've seen Sasha do a hundred times. Lily's mouth pulls into a smile, and I find myself mirroring the gesture as she talks to me in broken English I can mostly understand.

"I'm going to leave you guys to it," Lucy says, making her escape.

"Go easy on Lucy," Sasha says once the door snicks shut behind her. "She's used to being my protector."

I snort. I don't give a fuck what she's used to being, but for Sasha's sake I dial back the anger. I glance down at my daughter and that rage vanishes completely.

"I'm buying a house."

Her brows pull together. "Okay." She draws the word out, as if unsure where this is going.

"I want you and Lily with me."

I watch as her eyes soften. "I want that too, but what about Lucy? I can't just leave her. She took care of us all these—"

I silence her with a kiss. "I'll make sure she's taken care of. Let's get our girl her treatment and get her home."

SASHA

Tyler squeezes my hand for the third time in as many minutes. I know he's nervous. We both are. We're sitting in the hospital waiting area while Fury is in with the doctors and Whizz. So far, it's been quiet, but I'm braced for whatever might happen. The man might be a fierce bastard, but he's also shit-scared of needles, and they need to take a blood sample to confirm he's a match for Lily-May. I'm eager to get this side of things handled. I know a few days won't make a difference, but every second that ticks by feels like a second too long. I want my daughter well and fast.

"Should we be worried by the silence?" I ask, biting my bottom lip and wondering if Fury has gone on a killing spree.

Tyler cups my face and I manage to receive his touch without flinching in pain. It's been a week since Sin attacked me. My bruises are still ugly and prominent, but the cuts to my face are starting to scab over. I don't know if they'll scar, but I'm hopeful they won't. I don't want to have that constant reminder of that day looking back at me in the mirror, staring Ty in the face every time he looks at me.

"He'll do this," he says, and I smile, putting my faith in the man at my side.

Ty has been amazing the past few days. I didn't expect nightmares, but the first night Ty ordered me back to the clubhouse to rest, they came. I was back in that room with Sin and every dream ended with him raping me again, not being saved by Ty and the guys.

I know he's having his own dreams. He doesn't talk about it, but his sleep hasn't come easy. Nox told me it would stay with Ty for a while, what he did to Sin, but I hope he can eventually make peace with his decision. He deserves that.

"I know he'll do it. I just don't want him to kill Lily's doctor."

Ty snorts, but doesn't deny that could happen. It doesn't help my anxiety. A yell sounds from the room, and I brace. Shit. The sound of something knocking over has my unease going through the roof. Ty squeezes my hand again.

After a few moments, the door opens to the exam room, and I sit up straighter as Whizz comes out looking a little ruffled, Fury on his heels.

"Done?" Ty asks.

Whizz huffs out a breath, giving Fury a sidelong glare. "Yeah."

Fury holds a little cotton ball against the crook of his arm, his face pale. I come to my feet.

"There's not enough thank yous in the world for what you're doing for Lily-May."

His brows draw down at my words. "You're family."

My heart soars at his words. Family. Being accepted back into the fold by the brothers is a relief. I thought I lost my family after I left. Sin made me believe they'd never welcome me back. He was wrong. These lads have opened their arms and hearts to me as if I never left at all, and they've opened to

Lily-May too. I know she'll always have the protection of the club, and it makes me feel safer knowing that.

Whizz juts his chin at Fury. "You ready to head back to the clubhouse?"

He nods.

We watch them head for the exit before we make our way back to Lily-May's room. She's been doing well this week, better than usual, but she still needs the transplant desperately. I wish they would hurry things up. I can't bear seeing her in this place, suffering, but the doctors seem to be in control of things.

"Sash." He stops me before we go back into the room. I peer up at him, feeling my stomach flip at the seriousness of his expression.

"What?"

He pulls an envelope from the inside pocket of his kutte and taps it against his fingers.

"It's the paternity results. They came this morning."

My mouth dries and my heart rate starts to accelerate until I can barely get air down my windpipe.

"I don't need to see it."

"I already opened it."

I peer up at him. "You did?"

"I wanted to know first."

I try to swallow through the dryness, but I can't.

"And?"

He hands me the envelope. For a moment, I stare at it like it's live ammunition. I don't want to know the results, but if Tyler's seen it, I'm assuming the news is good. He would never have shown me this if it confirmed Sin was Lily-May's father.

Hope flares through me at that thought. I slowly pull the paper from the envelope and open it out. There's a load of science shit at the start I don't understand, so I skip to the main part of the letter, the part that says Lily-May is Tyler Jenkins' kid.

My heart canters in my chest as I read those words. I must have already been pregnant when Sin raped me. The thought makes me sick to my stomach, but relief also floods me knowing he doesn't have this final hold over me. That Lily won't be dirtied by what happened to me. She can love her father. She would never have been able to love Sin.

Tears well in my eyes and I let them fall unchecked. Tyler swipes them away with his thumb.

"She's mine."

"She's yours," I sob out and then he pulls me into a bone-crushing hug. His hand brushes over my hair as I cling to him, feeling my legs wobble beneath me.

"You're mine too."

I smile through my tears. "Always."

EPILOGUE

RAVAGE

TWO MONTHS LATER...

THE SMELL of meat cooking fills the air as soon as I step out of the car. My gaze moves across the compound towards the clubhouse, towards where the crowd of kuttes are gathered around the barbecue. From here, I can tell Titch and Levi are arguing over who is doing the cooking. I know because they have this same fucking debate during every monthly club cook out. Something about grilling meat outside brings the arsehole out in them both.

I shrug out of my kutte and turn it the right way around before settling it back onto my back just as Sasha climbs out of the car. My woman looks amazing tonight. She's wearing a pair of skin-tight jeans that should be fucking illegal, my property kutte and a tiny vest top beneath it that shows a slither of her stomach. The tattoo of Lily's name is visible on her wrist. The moment I laid eyes on her, I wanted to drag her upstairs and fuck her brains out, but we were already running late because of Lily-May.

My daughter does not like doing anything in a hurry.

She had the transplant a month ago. So far, it seems to have taken well, but it's still early days. All I know is my daughter has grown from strength to strength, completely changing from the sickly little girl in the hospital to a bubbly toddler with an attitude that reminds me of Sasha when she was young. She was only let out of the hospital this week and this is the first time we've taken her anywhere, so there are banners hanging from the walls of the building with 'welcome home' written on them. It warms me in a way I didn't think was possible to know my brothers have embraced my daughter the same way I have.

I move to the back door of the vehicle and pull it open. Lily-May peers up at me through long lashes and smiles a radiant smile that reminds me why I did all the shit I did, who I did it for. My family. And it feels amazing to be able to say that. I love them both. It's amazing how fast this little girl has wormed her way into my stone-cold heart. I didn't think I was capable of loving anyone, of letting anyone in but Sasha. Lily-May proved me wrong. The love I have for this little girl scares me sometimes.

Being responsible for her scares me.

I unfasten the straps in her car seat and pull her out of it, into my arms, tugging down the Untamed Sons tee she's wearing. When I start to lower her to the ground, she grips my neck, making me chuckle. I straighten, and she circles my neck tighter.

Holding out my other hand, Sasha takes it and together the three of us walk over to join my brothers.

"Hey! Look who's here!" Titch yells, a pair of tongs in his hands. He tickles under Lily's chin and she giggles a high-pitched sound that makes the ice around my heart thaw a little more.

"Really, Titch?" Sasha says, gesturing towards him even as

she rolls her eyes at him. He's wearing an apron with a picture of tits and a snatch on it.

"What?" he demands, holding his arms out as he peers down at himself.

She shakes her head at him, but there's a smirk on her lips. Sasha grew up here. She knows what the guys are like. Lily will probably learn a few new words from the brothers, but each one of them would die for her.

Nox strides over and hands a bottle of beer each to Sasha and me.

"Food should be done in a few, if those two dickheads can stop arguing for five seconds."

I don't care about the food. All I care about is the people here. My family by choice.

I let Lily-May down and she rushes over to Fury. She's taken a shine to him, although I don't think he knows how the hell to handle it. He stiffens but then after a moment is taken in by her raised hands, demanding he picks her up. He leans down and sweeps her up and I find myself grinning as she chatters a million miles per hour at him.

I move over to a bench, taking Sasha with me, one eye on my daughter as Sasha sits and talks to Briella, Levi's sister and Francesca, Daimon's cousin. Titch's boys, who are seven and five, are running around making bike noises, racing each other.

After a few moments, Fury puts her down and I stiffen as I watch her scampering over in our direction, my heart in my throat until she's at my side.

She surprises the fuck out of me by yelling, "Catch me!"

Then she throws herself into my arms and I'm glad I have fucking good reflexes. I wrap my arms around her and pull her to me, kissing her head.

"Daddy!"

I freeze. She's never called me that before. I wasn't

entirely sure she understood when Sasha was trying to tell her who I am.

I glimpse Sasha behind her who is grinning like crazy. "Yeah, baby. He's your daddy."

I hold my daughter close to me, breathing in her baby shampoo and powder smell, and Sasha grips my hand.

"I got something for you," I tell her.

She frowns. "What?"

I dig in my pocket around Lily-May and pull out a set of keys.

Her eyes flare. "Is that—"

"The keys to our new house."

Sasha comes to my side and dips down so she can press her mouth to mine.

"I love you."

"I love you too."

The roar of an engine catches my attention, and I move quickly, putting myself between my daughter, woman and the danger, fear clogging my arteries as a car peels through the gates, taking them off their hinges with a creak that hurts my ears. It crashes into a stone pillar at the side of the drive, the sound so loud it reverberates around the compound like an explosion.

Smoke pours from under the hood, making it hard to see what's going on. I hand Lily to Sasha and keep them both behind me as I reach around my back for my gun, ready to go to war with anyone here to harm my family.

"Get the women and children inside," I yell, knowing one of my brothers will see to it.

I see Sash, Briella, and the other women clamouring towards the clubhouse, Levi with them.

Kyle approaches the vehicle from the gate's security booth, gun drawn. The other brothers move closer, their own weapons aimed at the car.

Yells go up as my brothers shout instructions as they move to the car to see what the hell is going on. I can't see shit past the airbag which has deployed, smothering the occupant of the vehicle.

Nox moves like a panther next to Fury, gun raised, signalling to the others to close in.

The car door opens with a creak of protest and someone falls out of the driver's seat. All I see is blood, a fuck ton of it, but she's female. I can see that much.

Titch curses and cocks the hammer back on his firearm.

Nox moves forwards, then something dawns in his eyes and he stops.

"Fuck! Lower your guns!" Nox yells, "Lower your fucking guns."

Then he's moving and is in front of the car.

"Lucy?"

She peers up at him through the blood covering her, as if she's struggling to focus on him.

"Help."

The End

GET A FREE BOOK AND EXCLUSIVE CONTENT

Dear Reader,

Thank you so much for taking the time to read my book. One of my favourite parts of writing is connecting with you. From time to time, I send newsletters with the inside scoop on new releases, special offers and other bits of news relating to my books.

When you sign up, you'll get a free book.

Find out more here:

www.jessicaamesauthor.com/newsletter

Jess x

ENJOYED THIS BOOK?

Reviews are a vital component in any authors arsenal. It enables us to gain more recognition by bringing the books to the attention of other readers.

If you've enjoyed this book, I would be grateful if you could spend five minutes leaving a review on the book's store page. You can jump right to the page by clicking below:

https://books2read.com/Ravage-USMC

Have you read them all?

IN THE UNTAMED SONS MC SERIES

Ravage

Leaving Rav was the hardest decision I've ever had to make, but I didn't have a choice. Staying and facing my past wasn't an option. I suffered through hell, but I'm stronger than I've ever been, at least I was until my daughter got sick. Now, the only person left who might be able to save her is her father. Only, I have no idea who it is. Ravage, or his brother, Sin.

Download here: https://books2read.com/Ravage-USMC

Nox

Nox is falling for me, but he shouldn't. I have secrets and if he knew the truth he'd drop me in a heartbeat. The problem is I'm falling for him too, but when my past comes out he's going to hate me. Nothing is as it seems. My whole life is a lie. Everything except Nox. Because the truth is Lucy Franklin doesn't really exist.

Download here: https://books2read.com/Nox-USMC

IN THE LOST SAXONS SERIES

Snared Rider

A decade ago Beth fled Kingsley for one reason and one reason only: Logan Harlow. Sure, the man is a sex on legs biker, but he's also a thief; he stole her heart and broke it. Now, she's back in town and has no choice but to face him.

Download here: https://books2read.com/SnaredRider

Safe Rider

A new life; a new start—that was what Liv needed after escaping her violent marriage. Moving to Kingsley was a chance to show the world she wasn't defeated by her past. No part of that plan involved falling in love with a biker.

Download here: https://books2read.com/SafeRider

Secret Rider

A one-night stand—that was all she was supposed to be. She wasn't supposed to walk into his bar a week later and demand a job. Wade is used to dealing with formidable women but Paige may just be his match. She's fiery, feisty and he wants her, but before they can be together, he needs to learn what she's hiding.

Download here: https://books2read.com/SecretRider

Claimed Rider

(A Lost Saxons Short Story)

Liv survived a nightmare. She may have got her happily ever after, but things are still not perfect in her world. How can she prove to Dean that she's his in every way that matters?

Download here: https://books2read.com/ClaimedRider

Renewed Rider

Beth knows she has to fix things before her family is destroyed and she knows the only way to do that is with Logan at her side. Together, can they renew the bonds of brotherhood and rebuild the club before it's too late?

Forbidden Rider

The Lost Saxons stole Piper's future. They took her brother from her, put him on a bike and made him one of their own. Hating them was easy—until she met Jem Harlow. He's irritating beyond belief, pushy, charming, attractive, and he knows it. And he won't leave her alone. Worse still, she's falling for his act. There's only one problem: her brother does not want her anywhere near his club friends.

Christmas Rider

(A Lost Saxons Short Story)

Christmas in Kingsley should be a time for celebration, but with a maniac on the loose and a private investigator dogging their steps, things are tense as the festive season gets underway.

Flawed Rider

Noah 'Weed' Williams is not a good man. He drinks too much, sleeps around too much, and he doesn't think he's worthy of a meaningful relationship. Meeting Chloe opens his eyes to a world he could have, but he knows she deserves better than him.

Fallen Rider

Mackenzie is falling for the wrong man. Dane is completely off-limits, but she can't keep her mind off him. Running out on him after a one-night stand, she hoped she could avoid him, but fate has other ideas. When she's sent to his clubhouse for her own protection, she's put front and centre in his world and has no choice but to face up to her feelings for the man.

Download here: https://books2read.com/FallenRider

STANDALONE BOOKS

Match Me Perfect

He's a fisherman, she's a marketing manager. He lives on an island, she lives in London. Can online dating really match two people from different worlds?

Download here: https://books2read.com/MatchMePerfect

Stranded Hearts

(Love, Unexpected Collection)

Rhys Hale is a first-class jerk. Everything about him makes Zara's head want to explode. When he comes to her village, intending to put a stonking big development in the middle of it, the gauntlet is thrown down. The last thing she expected was for nature to play dirty and get stuck with him.

Download here: https://books2read.com/StrandedHearts

ABOUT THE AUTHOR

Jessica Ames lives in a small market town in the Midlands, England. She lives with her dog and when she's not writing, she's playing with crochet hooks.

For more updates join her readers group on Facebook:
www.facebook.com/groups/JessicaAmesClubhouse

Subscribe to her newsletter:
www.jessicaamesauthor.com

- facebook.com/JessicaAmesAuthor
- twitter.com/JessicaAmesAuth
- instagram.com/jessicaamesauthor
- goodreads.com/JessicaAmesAuthor
- bookbub.com/profile/jessica-ames

Printed in Great Britain
by Amazon